THICKER THAN WATER

THICKER THAN WATER

Carla Jablonski

razOr
bill

Thicker than Water

RAZORBILL

Published by the Penguin Group
Penguin Young Readers Group
345 Hudson Street, New York, New York 10014, U.S.A.
Penguin Group (USA) Inc., 375 Hudson Street, New York, New York 10014, U.S.A.
Penguin Group (Canada), 90 Eglinton Avenue, Suite 700, Toronto, Ontario,
Canada M4P 2Y3 (a division of Pearson Penguin Canada Inc.)
Penguin Books Ltd, 80 Strand, London WC2R 0RL, England
Penguin Ireland, 25 St Stephen's Green, Dublin 2, Ireland
(a division of Penguin Books Ltd)
Penguin Group (Australia), 250 Camberwell Road, Camberwell,
Victoria 3124, Australia (a division of Pearson Australia Group Pty Ltd)
Penguin Books India Pvt Ltd, 11 Community Centre, Panchsheel Park,
New Delhi - 110 017, India
Penguin Group (NZ), Cnr Airborne and Rosedale Roads, Albany,
Auckland 1310, New Zealand (a division of Pearson New Zealand Ltd)
Penguin Books (South Africa) (Pty) Ltd, 24 Sturdee Avenue, Rosebank,
Johannesburg 2196, South Africa

Penguin Books Ltd, Registered Offices: 80 Strand, London WC2R 0RL, England

10 9 8 7 6 5 4 3 2 1

Library of Congress Cataloging-in-Publication Data

Jablonski, Carla.
  Thicker than water / Carla Jablonski.
    p. cm.
  Summary: Coping with her mother's cancer makes seventeen-year-old Kia feel out of
place everywhere until she is drawn into the goth-vampire club scene, where she finds
acceptance and one gorgeous, popular guy who might offer escape.
  ISBN 1-59514-023-9
  [1. Goth culture (Subculture)—Fiction. 2. Cancer—Fiction. 3. Family problems—
Fiction. 4. Self-mutilation—Fiction. 5. High schools—Fiction. 6. Schools—Fiction.
7. New York (N.Y.)—Fiction.] I. Title.
  PZ7.J1285Thi 2006
  [Fic]—dc22

                                                          2005023868

Printed in the United States of America

For Jack K. and Rich O. for different reasons
and
For Liesa A. and Eloise F. for support, Shiraz, and smarts

PROLOGUE

The feeling threatened to overwhelm her. That intense throbbing in her veins, the area midway up the arm where several tributaries branched off. Or came together; she wasn't sure. They vibrated; it was almost as if she could hear them hum. No—she would resist, she wouldn't do it, not anymore.

The sensation stayed with her all afternoon. She went for a walk after school, hurtling past shops, trying to find something to look at, searching for distraction. She walked fast, then faster toward the brisk autumn sunset, trying to keep the sun up, dreading darkness.

At dinner she alternated between silence, so focused on hiding the yearning of her forearms, and talking too loudly, trying to drown out the sound of need. Her dad didn't notice. Just a mood, just her, just a teenage girl going through stuff.

They went their separate ways—her father to watch a game on TV, she to her improvised room.

Homework loomed and beckoned her, but it was a false offer, a cover. She knew closing her door was dangerous; she did it anyway. Books pulled from her bag, notebooks opened, pen at the ready. She stared at the blue lines on the loose-leaf page. She shrugged, took in breath, stood up, turned on the TV, and still she could feel her veins filling, rushing, circulating.

She went into the bathroom and splashed water on her face, gazed into her hooded eyes in the mirror. What was it? Why the drive, the pull? Why tonight? Was there even a trigger anymore or was her body making demands all on its own?

She could hear music far away—down on the street, out the bathroom window, and echoed in a counterpoint in the living room from her dad's TV. There was a tinny sound coming from her own television and then shouting when it changed to a commercial. What she heard more clearly was a pounding in her temples, an oceanic roar in her ears. Tense tense tense. She wanted to cry and couldn't—no tears would come; she even tried to force them. She didn't know where this deep agitation came from, but she sure knew how to get rid of it.

She flipped open the medicine cabinet, erasing her reflection by leaving the cabinet open, the mirror facing the wall. She yanked out the razor, gripped the pink plastic disposable with her right hand, squatted on the floor, straightened out her left arm, and held it steady between her knees.

She still had a moment not to do it, but she couldn't come up with any reason not to. Her breathing became deeper but faster and she dragged the razor against her arm. She had to angle it so that the sharp edge could cut her skin, challenging to manage with a disposable razor. That was the promise she had made herself—she would never use naked blades again. That promise she could keep. She plunged it against her skin over and over, not really seeing, just experiencing the welcome release, the rise of the blood filling the lines, the inside moving outside, the invisible being made visible; it was like magic. *Come out come out wherever you are.* First a thin white line, then the growing color marking the traces she'd made. Making it manifest. Present in the world. Ah, release. Then the final dispersing of energy so that she could stop. She was done.

She slumped against the bathtub, spent and satisfied. Her breathing came more regularly, less frantic, less labored. Good. That was good. But even as the word *good* entered her head, its opposite appeared. Shame crept into her and she flung the pink plastic tool skittering across the tile floor.

ONE

I s that what you're wearing?"

Kia didn't say a word. Why should she? It was an act. Her dad made the noises, affected the postures: bingo! Instant parent. He didn't *really* care that she had on heavy buckled black boots, fishnets, a gauzy black skirt, and a long-sleeved black T-shirt sporting the message I Bite. He knew the *form* of parental concern: *Parents comment on clothes, he comments on clothes, therefore he is a parent.* It was their little morning ritual that he express some semblance of involvement. No delving into her personal life (not that she'd talk to him about that kind of stuff), no checking on her slipping grades, no looking through her portfolio to be sure she was keeping up, no asking about her mom. Clothes were a battle without casualties.

She decided to play along: a shrug was her response. That was enough.

Her dad laughed and breezed through the dining room on

his way to his study—which was now her bedroom. "Well, I guess it could be worse. At least you don't look like a hooker like your friend Marni."

Kia took a bite of her bagel and wondered if she should tell him Marni wasn't her friend anymore. Nah. His remark was standard Parental Comment Number Seven. She thought of various replies: "I could try that look tomorrow." "Marni has the bod for it; I don't." "Shut up." But she chose, "Hey, I've got my standards."

Her dad grinned. "I know, kiddo. And thank God for that."

Morning contact completed. Good deed for the day.

It had been like this for three weeks now. Three weeks since Kia had packed her laptop, art supplies, and a pile of clothes and moved in with her father. Before that she'd spent the last five years, since her parents' divorce, seeing him every other weekend. Less, once Kia's own life became full with school and friends and projects. He didn't seem to mind—he hadn't wanted shared custody in the first place.

Not that he didn't love her in that global way that parents loved their kids. It was a given, right? Kia could see that. But she could also see she was in his way, and he was in hers.

Oh no. Kia's hand froze halfway to her mouth. He was in her bedroom—would he also go into her bathroom? Were there signs left from last night's slip? The bloodstained tissues that she had wrapped around her forearm—flushed. Nothing weird about the tossed Lady Sleek in the wastebasket. Not that he would even notice.

Holding up her hand, she pulled the fabric of her sleeve uncomfortably across her latest tracks. She put the bagel back onto the plate and eased the fabric away from her skin, wincing. She was out of practice. *I used to have this stuff down cold.* She couldn't risk loose sleeves because they could flop up and expose her and that was the last thing she wanted. But sleeves this tight could chafe her raw skin and maybe even start her bleeding again.

Dad crossed back in, having retrieved several folders from Kia's "bedroom."

"So," he said, flipping through some folders before stuffing them into his briefcase, "plans after school?"

Kia cleared her throat. A crumb scratched on its way down. "Hospital," she said. She coughed.

"Ah." Her dad didn't look at her, just fiddled with more papers. Arranging. Re-arranging. "Right." He snapped the brief-case shut. "I'll probably be late tonight."

He patted his jacket for his glasses, nodded, then felt his back pocket for his wallet and nodded again. Kia could remember him going through this routine ever since, well, ever since she could remember *him*. She always imagined that he was silently saying the word *check* after every pat and nod.

He smiled at her, obviously satisfied that he was set for the day. "Can you fend for yourself for dinner?"

"Yeah, no biggie." Kia took another bite of the bagel. "I can grab something at the hospital."

Her dad's brown eyes flicked away.

"And even if the hospital cafeteria food sucks," Kia contin-ued as she chewed, "there are loads of cafés and restaurants and stuff around the hospital." For some reason, Kia felt like saying "hospital" as many times as she could before her dad left for work. Maybe because she was the only one who ever went, and she needed to make the place real to him, the way it was for her.

Only it wasn't. All that real. More like super-real, like it was the only true reality and everything outside that noisy, airless building full of pain was fake, a time-out.

It might have been easier to go if it weren't a hospital where most people didn't get better. Specializing in cancer meant that they had the best staff, best surgeons, best specialists, best blah blah blah, but it sure made it hard on the visitors, knowing that every frail person strolling down a corridor in a blue gown wasn't likely to survive. Every child in a wheelchair was facing a probable death sentence. At least in other hospitals you went in to get cured, you went in to have babies—you went in anticipating coming out. But the place where Kia's mom was, most of what they did was maintenance. Pausing in the process toward dying.

Not always, Kia reminded herself. *Not every time. She came out before.*

Kia pushed the plate away, leaving half the bagel, and got up.

"You finished?" her dad said.

"Yeah." Before he could say anything annoying, like "breakfast is the most important meal of the day," Kia grabbed her backpack and left for school.

Aces. Made it out of the building without having to deal with some neighbor in the elevator. Often Kia skipped the elevator ride and clomped down the fire stairs. Her dad's apartment was on the Upper East Side, where the kids all went to private school, and small children were never taken there by actual parents but by nannies of other ethnic groups. Kia's dad had moved up in the world since the divorce, while she and her mom had been lucky just to hold steady.

She'd been in the apartment plenty of times before it had become her new address, of course, but now that she was fully ensconced, the differences between her and the rest of the people in the neighborhood were glaring. She stood out walking down the street—long multi-toned hair, all-black clothes, pierced eyebrow, nose stud, heavy-duty makeup were rarities on the Upper East Side.

At least there was one benefit from her temporary headquarters at Dad's, she thought as she scratched off a flyer pasted inside the bus shelter. No early morning subway ride. Kia went to a nearby public school that specialized in music and art. She had always hated the subway ride from her mom's funky little apartment in the West Village.

The bus arrived and Kia squeezed her way to the back. She plopped into a seat and stared out the window at the gray world. The windows on the bus were surprisingly clean, but the late September drizzle and fog turned everything outside impressionistic. Fuzzy. Like her thoughts.

This sluggishness was a familiar feeling. The morning-after uglies. Back when she was hitting the blades regularly, this was always the aftermath. Today, though, there was an added undercurrent of bewilderment. She had managed to stop for such a long time.

Kia couldn't remember the first time she took a razor blade to her skin. It had begun with her nails, scratching herself with a violence she didn't recognize. At some point she graduated to blades. What she remembered most clearly were her attempts to stop. The shame and fear she felt—what kind of freak *does* this kind of thing? But she also recalled with absolute clarity the sense of release and relief the cutting provided.

She'd quit because ultimately the tugging stopped or at least lessened enough for her to get control back somehow. Until last night.

But why? Why was it back now? Her mom had been diagnosed six months ago—she hadn't done it then. Her mom was back in the hospital three weeks later—she didn't start then. And since she didn't really understand how she had managed to stop last time, she wondered if she'd just keep on doing it now.

Not until she died or anything. Suicide was not appealing, nor was it the reason she sliced her skin. And this was no "cry for attention," since to get attention for it, someone would have to know and no one did. Kia made sure of that.

Kia rolled her hands up so she could tug her sleeves down a little farther onto her wrists. The cuts were higher up: they ran the length of the veins from the inside of her elbow to just above the cuff of her shirt. Even in the throes of the cutting, she knew where to stop. Kia smirked. *I'm the most in-control out-of-control person I know.*

The bus pulled up to her stop and Kia got off and joined the packs of kids heading into school.

"Hey, Gloomy!" A tall, scrawny redheaded guy banged into Kia so hard she nearly tripped.

"Aaron," Kia scolded, pulling her bag back up onto her shoulder.

"I called your name like three times before I hip-checked you back into this world," Aaron said. "Everything okay?"

"I'm not gloomy," Kia said. "Just . . . thinking." She did her best to stretch her mouth into a grin. "But now that I'm at school, I won't have to think anymore, will I?"

"Oh no, thinking is highly frowned upon here!" Aaron said. "And if you indulged in such an activity, you'd be in the minority anyway."

"So, really, why the cheer?" Kia asked. She fluffed up her bangs while examining her reflection in the glass window of the entrance doors. Her thick dark eyeliner was drawn expertly, no wobbly lines, and just the right amount to make her look intense but not raccoonish. Her purple-black lipstick created the perfect pout with no going outside the lines at all and no smudging. Mornings after, she tended to be extremely meticulous.

Her outfit had been chosen for comfort and camouflage. She tended toward layers—all in various shades of black—and today, with the requisite long sleeves. Kia was tall, with definite curves, and liked the way loose clothing sort of kept her shape hidden. She wasn't fat, but next to skinny Aaron and their slim friend Carol, it was hard not to feel big.

"I have plans for tonight—and not just for me," Aaron said. He pushed open the door and they went into the building. "For you and Carol too."

"I'm supposed to go to the hospital today," Kia said.

"That's okay; this is a night thing. And since it's Friday, there's no backing out because it's a weeknight. Not even from our overly conscientious Carol."

"And what is this nighttime thing?" Kia asked.

"Tell you at lunch!" Aaron called before being swallowed by the swarm of kids finding their homerooms. Kia saw him wave hello to some of the other students in the music program, then she turned and headed for her classroom.

"Hey," a boy sitting in the back row greeted Kia as she slid into her seat next to him. Virgil had choppy hair dyed as black as Kia's and three studs in his ear. His leather jacket had a skull and crossbones on the back. He was tilted back in his chair and his sturdy boots, similar to Kia's, were up on his desk.

"Hey, Virgil," Kia replied.

Virgil thudded the front legs of his chair back onto the floor and rummaged in his backpack. He pulled out a CD and tossed it onto Kia's desk. "Made this for you."

Kia picked up the CD. "What is it?"

He shrugged. "More of those bands you liked. I was trolling through some MP3 stuff and burned you some."

"Thanks. I liked the last one you gave me."

Virgil grinned, flashing his dimples. He didn't smile that much and suddenly she wondered if it was because he knew that the dimples made him look really sweet, like a goth cherub. His smile definitely took the edge off his hard-core image. So did his personality, but Kia didn't want to break it to him that for all his swagger, he was actually nice.

She slipped the CD into her bag as Ms. Romero walked in and took attendance. One good thing about school: Kia wouldn't have to worry about a slip for a whole six hours.

Kia was hit by a wave of noise as she entered the cafeteria. Was it something about the Formica surfaces and hard plastic that made sound reverberate? She nodded hello to Marni and the rest of her old group of friends, the ones she never talked to anymore. It wasn't like they'd started being mean to her or any-thing—they just got distant. As if her mom's cancer were con-tagious or after all the drama of the diagnosis, before the summer and the first round of chemo, they just didn't know how to deal with Kia anymore. Maybe it was all just too boring. It was sometimes boring to Kia.

She easily spotted Aaron's lanky frame and red hair loping through the maze of tables. Aaron had grown six inches over the summer without putting on a single pound (at least it looked that way), so he really stood out in the crowd. Unfortunately, a glimpse of his face did the trick too since acne had recently taken hold of his skin like an invading army. Aaron sat down at a table near the windows with the third member of their trio, Carol Avery.

Carol's long auburn hair was backlit by the dim rays struggling to get through the grime on the chicken-wired windows. Carol was like a cat—she always managed to position herself in the most flattering, photogenic spots completely unselfconsciously.

Carol was in the music program with Aaron—she was a flute player and also had a light soprano voice. But she and Kia had been friends long before high school. They had grown up in the same neighborhood, so they had gone to the same middle school together too. Not long ago, Carol's older brother had dropped out of college and run away: a different kind of grief than Kia knew, but for both of them loss was always possible, always hov-ering. As a result Kia and Carol shared a similar anxiety around telephone rings. They communicated mostly by e-mail.

"Hey, you," Aaron greeted Kia as she dropped into the seat beside Carol.

"Aaron has plans for us," Carol said.

Kia raised her pierced eyebrow. "I heard. And what might they be?"

"Do you know what today is?" Aaron asked.

"Friday," Carol replied. "As in thank God it's."

"True. But it's also the autumnal equinox. Very important day in the witchy world."

"And this matters to us because . . . ?" Kia asked.

"Because there is going to be a public Mabon ceremony tonight in Central Park, and we're going to be there," Aaron explained.

"What kind of ceremony?" Kia asked.

"Pay attention! It's a Wiccan ceremony celebrating the autumnal equinox. You know, witches."

"Like for Halloween?" Carol asked.

Aaron rolled his eyes. "No. There are real people who practice witchcraft all over the city all year round."

"But are they people we actually want to know?" Kia asked.

"Of course they are! They're mysterious. And interesting!" Aaron waggled his strawberry blond eyebrows. "And maybe cute guys will be there. For all of us."

"Why didn't you say that in the first place?" Carol asked.

Kia laughed. Carol was always on the lookout for new playmates. She divided her time between intense studying and even more intense make-out sessions, but her primary emphasis was always on the academics. Those two interests left her little time for anything else, including friends. Aaron and Kia were the rare exceptions.

"Sounds fun." Carol turned to Kia. "What do you think?"

Kia knew going with them would be safer than being home alone after her slip last night, but the whole fake witch ritual sounded pretty lame.

"Well?" Aaron prodded. "I know you're going to the hospital, but the event starts at sunset. Hang with your mom for an hour and then head over. It's on the east side of the park anyway."

"Yeah, maybe," Kia hedged.

Carol glanced at Kia. "How's that going, with your mom?" she asked.

Kia shrugged.

"And your dad still never goes with you?" Aaron asked. Kia knew he was really pissed at Kia's dad for not being very involved during her mom's first stint in the hospital six months ago, when she had been diagnosed and had surgery. Kia was pissed too, but it wasn't like there was anything she could do about it.

It was scary. You loved someone enough to marry them, have a kid even, but in spite of all that, somewhere along the way you got to a point where not even a life-threatening illness could bring about the courtesy of a phone call.

"You know Dad," Kia said to Aaron. "Intense stuff has never been his thing."

"True," Carol said, sipping a diet soda. "Like when you had to get stitches. He spent more time threatening lawsuits against the playground than taking care of you."

Kia laughed. "Exactly. Ruling the co-op board in his building and eating in nice restaurants. Those are his specialties."

The bell rang, and Kia finished her soda.

"So?" Aaron asked. "We on for later?"

"Sure," Kia said. "Why not?"

For the rest of the afternoon, Kia blurred through her classes. She never felt pulled into focus, probably a result of her close encounter of the razor blade kind the previous night. She stashed her stuff in her locker when the final bell sounded and headed for the exit.

She was just outside the door when it hit her that she'd totally forgotten about ceramics class. A thick guy with a thicker backpack slammed into her when she skidded to a stop.

"Hey," he snarled. "Watch out."

"Sorry," Kia said, scurrying back into school.

She raced around a corner, realizing that if she went to the hospital after ceramics, she'd have to miss the Wicca ceremony.

She could always skip the hospital visit today. It wasn't like she'd be able to have an extended visit like she could over the weekend.

Visiting hours are till nine, she reminded herself as she strode into the ceramics classroom and found her spot at the long table.

"Hey, want to grab some fries after this?" Virgil was standing next to her, scraping tool tucked behind a pierced ear.

Kia had been surprised when Virgil showed up in the first ceramics class. Everyone in the art program pretty much had to take some after-school elective, so he had to be *somewhere*. Still . . . ceramics?

He was trying to invent the perfect coffee mug. So far, none had made it into the kiln.

"Huh?" Kia said. "Did you say something about being fried?"

"Eat food. Post this."

"Oh. Yeah, sure."

Why did she say that? She already had more plans than she could fit after school.

Kia turned back to her vase. It was small, meant to hold a single flower. She was having trouble with the neck.

Now she really needed to re-schedule the hospital visit. She dipped her fingers into a bowl of water and ran them over the clay. *Mom will understand,* she thought. She'd made some comment yesterday about Kia spent too much time at the hospital anyway. Kia worked the neck, trying to make it more pliable.

Class over, and Virgil and Kia left the building. The art side of the building always had a faint mist of paint and plaster smells, and Virgil lit up a cigarette as soon as they stepped outside. Kia's nose wrinkled in reaction to all the competing smells.

"Nikko's?" Virgil asked. "Or Diner?"

Nikko's was the pizza place across the street. The diner was a few blocks away.

"I don't know," Kia said. "Can I borrow your cell first, though? I forgot mine, and I just have to make a quick call."

"Sure." Virgil unclipped his much-adored phone from his belt loop and handed it over. His eyes stayed glued to the little silver object.

"I promise I won't hurt it," Kia said.

Virgil blushed, proving that a pale goth complexion wasn't necessarily a good thing. No camouflage. No protective coloring.

Note to self: Even with all the cool, and the black, the piercings, and the tattoos, the face can still betray you.

She punched the numbers for her mom's hospital room. It only rang once before her mother answered. "Hello?"

Kia winced. Did her mother pick up so fast because she was sitting there waiting?

"It's me. Listen, uh, I think I'm not going to be able to come by today," Kia said. She tugged at the hair at the nape of her neck.

"Oh, that's okay, honey," her mom said.

Off the hook! At the burst of elation Kia felt immediately guilty.

"Are you sure?" Kia asked. "I mean, I actually could come if you want me to. It's just there's some stuff. . . ."

"No, really. Go do what you want to do. It's too nice a day to be cooped up in here. Unless you're hooked up to an IV and they won't let you out."

"Uh, yeah." Kia wasn't ever sure how to take what Dad called her mom's "gallows humor."

"Will you . . ." Her mother hesitated for a minute. "Will you be around this weekend?"

Kia's face flushed. She never should have canceled.

"Of course," Kia assured her mother too loudly. She felt Virgil's surveillance change. She could tell he had become focused on more than just his precious and vulnerable cell phone. "I can even come now if—"

"No, no, tomorrow will be fine. Or Sunday. Whenever works for you."

"Tomorrow," Kia promised. They clicked off.

"One more?" Kia asked Virgil. His head was cocked and he just nodded.

"Hey, Dad," Kia said when her father answered the phone. "I'm going to hang out with Aaron and Carol tonight."

"That's good since I'll be out somewhat late myself. Are you staying over at Carol's?"

"I don't know." Kia didn't want to make it easy for her dad by staying out all night. On the other hand, if she went home, she might slip again. Staying at Carol's would be safer. "I'll let you know." There. Nice and ambiguous. Now he couldn't bring back some babe in case Kia walked in, but if she didn't sleep at home, he'd wish he had. A two-pronged psych-out.

She clicked off again and handed the phone back to Virgil.

"Thanks."

"Yeah. So did you decide? Pizza or fries?"

"I don't care. I just want a soda anyway."

"Pizza. Why hunt and gather when you can just fall into a plastic chair?"

They crossed the street and were assaulted by an overpowering garlic smell wafting through the small, hot space.

"Good thing we're not vampires," Virgil joked. "We'd have just been expelled forcibly."

They slid into a booth with plastic orange cushions. "Seriously? No pizza?" Virgil looked at her. "My treat."

"Did you just come into an inheritance?" Virgil was notoriously cheap. He never offered to spend money on anyone. In fact, she should offer to pay for her phone charges. He kept track of stuff like that. He even charged her for the blank CDs when he burned anything for her—even though she never asked him to give her music.

Virgil shrugged. "Well, do you?"

"Uh, yeah, sure. A plain slice and a Diet Coke."

Virgil went up to the counter while Kia defended their booth, knowing if she vacated the table, she'd lose their spot as more kids piled in. She watched Virgil, frowning slightly, trying to figure out what was going on. Was this a date? Was that how you could tell, when the guy suddenly offered to treat?

Kia had made out with some guys, and last summer at art camp she had slept with one of the other junior counselors she'd sort of been going out with. But none of that seemed to help her figure out guys any more than when she had been a virgin.

At the counter, Virgil held up a paper plate and mimed shaking spices onto it. Kia shook her head no. He loaded up his slice with extra garlic and red pepper flakes.

Kia narrowed her eyes at his pepperoni, assessing. If this really was a date, he probably would have been more worried about garlic breath. She leaned back against the booth and drummed the table with her fingertips.

He sat opposite her and slid the plain pizza slice in front of her. She unwrapped a straw and swirled it around in the Diet Coke, watching the ice cubes dance.

"So it must be really weird," he said.

"What?" Kia took a sip of the soda.

"You know, with your mom."

Kia's ears felt cold. She stared at the deep maroon lipstick on the tip of her straw. He wasn't really going to talk about *that*, was he?

She looked him straight in the eye. "What about my mom?" she asked. *I dare you,* she thought.

"Well, you know. Being sick."

"It's not *weird*; people get sick every day. There's nothing at all unusual about it."

"I just meant—"

"What's weird is how other people act about it."

Now Kia looked down. But her face was still neutral. It was Virgil's that was showing too much. So much that Kia didn't want to see. She'd stung him and it was hard to watch his struggle to find how to respond.

Go ahead. Dig yourself out. You'll get no help from me.

"I don't mean to be acting weird." Virgil's voice was softer than Kia had expected. "That's the point. Why I mentioned it. So you could tell me how to not act weird."

Kia snorted. "How much time you got? That's a looong list. Lots of making over to do. For starters, lose the notebook where you write down what people owe you."

"Kia, look." Now he sounded annoyed. "My parents are budget freaks and I have to show them *on paper* where I'm spending my money. Okay? Because they're afraid I'm spending money on drugs. That's the deal with *my* parents. But that doesn't tell me about the deal with yours. I have no idea what it would be like to have a mom who's dying. Which makes it hard to know the right things to say."

Kia's eyes narrowed to slits. "Start by getting your facts straight, asshole. My mother is not dying."

She banged her hands down on the table and stood up, accidentally knocking her pizza slice onto the floor. Facedown, of course. At least she missed her backpack and boots. She stepped over the mess and slammed out the door.

She immediately turned several corners so that if Virgil in some misguided attempt to make things better followed her, he wouldn't be able to. She hurried toward the park and didn't slow her pace till she hit the cover of the Tavern on the Green restaurant just inside the park entrance.

That total jerk! I can't believe I thought this was a date! It was pity pizza.
Kia strode deeper into the park, pausing to catch her breath by
the snack bar.

Kia banged the brick wall with one thick-booted foot over
and over. How dare he say that? He didn't know.

She stopped kicking. That's what they all thought. That's
why she was avoided. Why Marni and the others weren't her
friends anymore. No one could deal.

But her mom was going to get better. That's what no one
seemed to get. Cancer wasn't always a death sentence. Her mom
had beat it before, right? Other people got cured. Went into
remission. Her mother wasn't going to die. Not possible.

Kia crouched down and leaned against the bricks. *Stare into
space and don't see anything,* she instructed herself. *Soft lines, no hard
edges. Breathe. Breathe. Breathe.*

The smell of grilling meat distracted her, made her hungry.

She stood up and bought herself a hot dog. Fries too. She ate
as she walked, watching dog walkers and Frisbee players, moms
with kids, dads with kids, and kids with kids. She was supposed
to meet Aaron and Carol on the Great Lawn, so she headed in
that direction.

She was glad now that she'd decided to go to this witch
thing, even if it ended up being lame. She needed a way to get
that whole scene with Virgil out of her head.

Don't think about that, she told herself. *Think about . . . the rhythm of
your feet. Think of every shade that blue can be.*

Kia arrived at the top of the stairs leading down to Bethesda
Fountain. It always struck her as overly picturesque, fitting too
well in its landscape. She liked ragged views. This was too

designed. She could imagine someone standing in this spot to determine the position of the angel at the top so that it would be perfectly framed by distant foliage.

Kia avoided getting in the way of people taking pictures as she walked down the broad staircase to the plaza around the fountain, finally arriving at what she thought was the meeting place. Off to the edge of the lawn were three adults in long flowing caftan-type gear. One had a drum. As she watched, another taped a copy of the flyer Aaron had shown them to a nearby tree.

Kia sat on a bench to wait for her friends, staring into space.

What was she doing there? Waiting for some sort of supernatural intervention? Like that could happen.

Keep an open mind, Kia scolded herself. Life did have a way of surprising you. She just hoped her next surprise was a good one.

TWO

Kia stood flanked between Carol and Aaron. There was no way she was going to hold hands with any of these freaks—and she didn't need tarot cards to know that hand-holding was going to come up.

She forced herself to look around the circle again to find something—anything—positive. For some reason, Aaron was into this, and she loved Aaron, so she needed to give it a chance.

Carol was talking to the woman on the other side of her, discussing jewelry. The woman was tall and thin, wearing a bright orange turban. *She looks okay,* Kia thought, working hard to lose her judgmental stance.

About twenty people had gathered by now. Mostly women, older than Kia, but there were men scattered too. Dudes with beards and thinning hair that they wore long in back in pony-tails. The few kids Kia's age thankfully didn't go to their school. Kia did not want to be identified as one of these wacky Wiccans.

Not that she would be. Kia looked down at her outfit and then back around the group. Not much black in this crowd.

Aaron took Kia's hand and twisted it so that their thumbs pointed across the circle. "Check him out," he murmured. "My future husband."

Kia followed Aaron's gaze across the circle. Her friend's future husband was slight, with dark floppy curls that brushed his shoulders. He wore a blue turtleneck, faded jeans, and scuffed sneakers. His small nose and blue eyes, set wide apart, made Kia think of an elf. Not her type, but certainly cute—and definitely high school age.

Probably out of Aaron's league, Kia thought with a pang. At the moment, anyway. Aaron's body just needed to catch up with his height, and then when his skin cleared up, he'd be back to being a total cutie.

"I'd learn to cook for a boy like that," Aaron crooned.

"Aren't we supposed to be communing with the divine?" Kia teased. "Not cruising."

"Okay, so what's my game plan?" he said, ignoring Kia's comment, his words coming out rapid-fire. "You think I can get him to talk to me? Or maybe I shouldn't go that route—don't want to scare him off by actually meeting me. Should I play mysterious? Warm? Friendly? Cool?"

Kia couldn't have interrupted Aaron's stream of anxiety if she had tried, but the woman who seemed to be in charge managed. She stepped into the center of the circle and hit a drum. She was tall, with short brown hair, and looked about forty. She struck the drum again, and a hush settled over the circle.

"Let me begin by welcoming you all to our Mabon ceremony. I am Lady Aurora, priestess of the Coven of Light. We hold these rituals publicly to enlighten, to educate, to celebrate. We also use these circles to send and receive energy."

"Can we use her to get cable?" Kia whispered.

"Shh." Aaron hushed her.

"Tonight we will perform a ritual that draws from the wisdom of the Wheel of Life. We turn the wheel, and the natural cycle of life continues. All is order; all is right, even in seemingly random events."

Yeah, if you say so, Kia thought, holding back a derisive snort. Her deeply random life was so ordered.

There were smiles around the circle, some shut eyes, and definite excitement. Kia wondered if anyone else there felt as stupid as she did.

"We are at the moment when light and dark are equal," Lady Aurora said. "We are on the cusp of going into the dark. Before we do, we reap our harvest, for now what is manifesting in our lives is what we sowed in the previous quarter. Look to your own lives and see how you created that which you experience now."

Kia felt her stomach tighten. How could what she was going through be something she created? And what the hell could her mother have done that made cancer her "harvest"?

Kia tried to release her hands from Carol and Aaron's so she could break the stupid circle and walk out of there, but they both just tightened their grips.

Lady Aurora beat the drum regularly now. "At this pinnacle of balance, the sun diminishes and darkness takes over. We go into a time of turning inward and exploring this dark phase in all its aspects."

People were beginning to sway, and several started a low hum. Aaron looked at Kia and smiled broadly. Kia glanced at Carol, but Carol's eyes were closed.

A chant began. "Dark and light, life and death. Sow and reap." Still holding hands, they all began to slowly move around the circle.

Oh, great, Kia thought. *Now for the folk dancing.*

The drumming got louder as the chanting built, and everyone picked up speed. The circle became an oval, a parabola, an evolving elastic shape.

"Dark and light!" people shouted. "Life and death!" "Sow and reap!"

Kia could hear Aaron shouting and Carol's softer voice murmuring behind her.

"We prepare ourselves for the dark!" Lady Aurora shouted above the chant and the drums. "What will sustain you?"

"Goddess!" someone shouted.

"What will sustain you?" Lady Aurora cried again.

Kia was panting, her breath ragged as everyone continued to run, to twist, to jump. Her muscles felt good with the exercise, warming her in the darkening twilight.

"Fire sustains us!"

"The Great Mother!"

"What sustains you?" Lady Aurora's voice dropped to a deeper register so that it sounded like another drum. She repeated the phrase over and over under the thumping feet, the heavy breaths, the drumming, the shouting.

"Truth sustains us!" a woman cried.

"Love!" someone responded.

"Friends," Aaron yelled beside Kia. "Friends sustain us."

Now the drumming slowed down and the circle changed pace to match. Gradually the group was walking. Kia hated to admit it, but she actually felt better, energized.

She looked at Aaron, his blue eyes shining, a smile so broad it looked as if his ears were tugging on each side of his mouth. Carol's face was flushed a rosy pink, and her chest rose and fell with her deep breaths. The three squeezed hands as they came to a stop.

"With the energy we've raised, let us make a blessing to our Mother, the Earth who sustains us," Lady Aurora said. "We send out this loving energy to undo the harm our species wreaks upon this world. We are grateful for our bounty, and now as we go into the dark times, we bring with us the strength and energy of our circle."

Everyone released hands and most plopped onto the lawn. Kia pulled herself into a cross-legged position on the grass. Aaron sprawled beside her while Carol tucked her legs under herself.

"Wow!" Aaron said, the ear-to-ear grin still across his face. "That really was something."

Carol nodded. "I feel . . . different. What about you?"

Kia shrugged. "It was okay, I guess. I liked the aerobic portion of the program."

Aaron knocked into Kia's shoulder with his own. "Skeptic. Cynic. We shall cure you of these ills. Didn't you feel something?"

Kia looked at her friends. Their faces looked like matching moons, shining in the now-dark park, illuminated by the old-fashioned streetlamps just overheard. "Yeah . . ." Kia admitted slowly. "I felt something while we were dancing. Connected some way."

"Exactly!" Aaron's head bobbed up and down fervently.

"Would you like some apple cider?" One of the girls who looked their age held out a cup to Carol. She was carrying a thermos and a stack of cups. Her deep orange dress hung loosely over thick brown leggings, making her resemble an autumn leaf.

"Sure." Carol took one of the cups and held it out for the cider.

"I'm Steffi," the girl said. She flashed Aaron a smile of such wattage Kia wondered if she thought he was straight.

Kia reached up to take a cup from Steffi. She noticed the girl give her a once-over that was less welcoming than the warm smiles she had given Aaron and Carol.

Was it the nose stud? The eyebrow ring? *Or do I radiate a "my mom has cancer" aura?*

Steffi poured the cider and Kia watched the steam rise into swirls above the cup.

She sipped the drink as Steffi moved away.

Aaron sighed. "Isn't he beautiful?"

Kia glanced across the circle at Elf Boy, watching as he and Steffi exchanged friendly hellos. "So go talk to him," she said.

Aaron shuddered. "I can't."

"He keeps checking you out," Carol said. "Haven't you noticed?"

"I make a great impression from a distance," Aaron said. "But up close . . ." His voice trailed off.

Kia stood and grabbed his hand. "Okay, let's make you the best impression possible. Look interesting."

"What?"

"Let him see from over there just how dynamic, sexy, and in demand you are," Kia coached. "Say something."

"What are you doing?" Aaron asked.

She laughed and touched his arm. "I'm making it look as if you said something hilarious. Funny is attractive."

Carol stood too. She slipped her arm through Aaron's and beamed at him. "And I'm making it look as if I can't stand not being included because you are just too fun."

Aaron wriggled out of Carol's clutches. "Actually, you two are making me look straight—which is totally the *wrong* impression."

"Let's go talk to Steffi," Carol said. "She was friendly, and she seems to know him. She can tell him how charming you are."

"Oh, well, that's easy. I excel in situations of no sexual tension," Aaron said. He and Carol traipsed across the grass toward Steffi. They said something to her, then Elf Boy joined in the conversation, and everyone seemed to be having a good time.

"Productive?" Kia asked as Aaron and Carol wandered back to where she was standing.

"Very," Carol said.

"His name is Michael," Aaron gushed.

"I prefer Elf Boy," Kia said. "Can I call him that?"

"Sure," Aaron replied. "It can be his code name so we can talk about him secretly."

"I'm hungry," Carol said. She turned to Kia. "Are you sleeping over?"

"If that's okay, yeah," Kia said. She didn't feel ready to go home. "I have to let my dad know. But he can wait."

"Let's go eat," Aaron said.

Aaron and Carol waved goodbye to Steffi. Elf Boy waved back, causing Aaron to whirl around and walk away very quickly.

"Did you see that?" he asked, gripping Kia's arm.

"I think you've made a conquest," Carol said.

"And I think it was very smart to make this quick exit," Kia said. "Otherwise you might have actually waved back."

Aaron stopped dead. "Oh no." His eyes widened. "Do you think he thinks I'm rude?"

"I think he thinks you have someplace to go," Carol assured him.

"Which is also attractive," Kia said.

As they made their way through the darkened park, Kia noticed the crowds had thinned since her walk over.

"So do you think it's real?" Carol asked. "Magic. Witchcraft. Making things happen with rituals and spells?"

"Definitely," Aaron said. "I decided after the first season that *Buffy* wasn't just a TV show; it was a documentary."

"*Buffy* is mostly about vampires, not witches," Kia said. "So now you think vampires are real too?"

"I think everything is real if I say it's real," Aaron said.

"According to quantum physics, that's closer to right than you might think," Carol said.

"How's that work exactly?" Kia asked. They came around Bethesda Fountain and headed toward Strawberry Fields at the west side of the park.

"Well, there's this whole thing about how the observer affects the outcome," Carol explained. "Which means the physical world, even at the quantum level, is changeable and even controllable if you know what you're doing."

"So, what, my random thoughts are making things happen?" Kia asked.

"Well, we always suspected that thinking was dangerous," Aaron joked.

"Come on, guys," Carol said. "You're taking physics too."

"Yes, but you're the only one who pays attention," Aaron pointed out.

Carol shook her head. "There's also the rule that matter is never created or destroyed, but simply transformed."

"So you think there's science to all this occult stuff?" Kia asked. She wasn't sure if she liked that idea or if it just made her more freaked out about the world in general.

Carol shrugged as they left the park. "I'm just saying that the more I study quantum, the more I think magic is possible."

"And what about all those miracles you hear about?" Aaron said as they stopped for a traffic light. "You know, people praying for someone they don't know and then the sick person gets better."

Kia stiffened. Did Aaron want to get into this whole magic thing because of her mom?

"Wouldn't it be great? If we could really change things with magic?" Aaron said, his voice wistful.

"What would you change?" Kia asked cautiously.

"What do you think?" Aaron held up a hand and made a circling motion around his face.

Kia turned to Carol. "How about you?"

Carol's eyes stayed focused on the street ahead. "I'd do a magic spell to become visible."

"That's a twist," Kia said with a laugh. "Isn't *invisibility* a better power?"

"Besides," Aaron added, "you already are visible. We can see you."

"I mean to my parents." She pushed her long hair behind her ears and cleared her throat. "My brother sent a postcard from Chicago. All it said was, 'I'm alive.'"

Aaron was quiet for a second, then turned to Kia. "And you?"

Kia knew the question was coming. She tried to think of something to say, something other than, "I'd do a spell so that I never picked up a razor blade again."

Carol put a hand on Kia's arm. "We know what kind of spell you'd cast," she said softly. "Something to cure your mom."

Kia felt her face flush with shame. *On top of everything else that's wrong with me, add selfishness.* She smiled and nodded. "Well, yeah."

Aaron took her hand and squeezed. And Kia added, "And to be a better person."

That was a spell she seriously needed to find.

THREE

K ia stood by the silver elevators, picking at her black nail polish. A ding announced the elevator's arrival, and Kia stood aside to allow a blue-robed skeletal man exit with his IV pole. Her jaw tensed as she stepped into the elevator with a father carrying a small child and a Mylar balloon saying Get Well Soon, two doctors, and a Chinese food deliveryman. She leaned into the corner and pretended she wasn't there.

She arrived on her mom's floor and walked past the big desk where white-coated people conferred about life and death and deli menus. One nurse with a drawling southern accent was always nice, and once she realized that there was no husband/dad in the picture, she always took Kia's questions seriously. Not that Kia asked much. She didn't know what she ought to know and was pretty sure that knowing too much was not going to help. Mostly she wanted to be sure her mom had ice, and a vomit bucket, and got cleaned up, and wasn't being accidentally OD'd like patients sometimes were on TV.

"Hey, Mom," Kia said before she even passed the dividing curtain separating her mom from The Roommate. The door was always kept open and there was no point in knocking, so this allowed Kia to put on her practiced grin and force her voice into its cheery register.

"Hi, sweetie," her mom answered in a whispery voice.

Kia felt a sharp stab in her chest. Mom must have had her treatment recently.

Kia came around the curtain, wearing her smile as an uncomfortable accessory. "Hey, how's it going today?"

Kia settled under the fading Monet print. She slung a booted leg over the arm of the chair. She tried not to notice her mother's shape under the sheets: she'd lost weight since last week. The IV dripped into her arm and her head was wrapped in a turban. A cup of ice chips on the dresser next to the phone sweated condensation down its plastic pseudo-pink sides.

Why are there no clear colors in a hospital? Kia wondered. The uniforms had identifiable colors—the whites, the blues, the greens, the aggressively cheerful prints on the nurses' and aides' tops. But in the rooms, the wood wasn't real wood color—it had no depth, the hard plastic cups and barf buckets were a weird shade of maybe-mauve, the covers on the food trays weren't really white— not because they were dirty but because they'd *never* been white. It was all approximation of color, nothing intense, nothing vivid.

"Did you have a nice time yesterday?" Mom asked. Kia could see the effort she was making to form words.

"Yeah. I hung with Aaron and Carol," Kia said. She scanned the room. Her eyes lit on a newspaper. She stood and grabbed it from the low radiator along the window. "Is this today's?" she asked.

Her mother nodded slowly.

"Haven't seen it yet," Kia said. She sat on the radiator. "Should I read it to you?"

The corner of her mom's mouth lifted and she nodded again.

If she read, Kia didn't have to make eye contact. If she read, her mom wouldn't have to speak. If she read, she wouldn't have to think of something to say.

Kia made it through the entire Arts section, the front page, and was starting on local news, worrying that Saturday's newspaper didn't have enough sections. Sunday's would be better. She could probably read the Sunday paper for nearly a week.

A sharp knock came on the open door and a group of white coats entered. They bypassed The Roommate and yanked aside the curtain.

Kia stood up. "Lunch," she declared. "Didn't eat much break-fast," she said to her mom, ignoring the stethoscope adjustments, the IV readings, the clipboard clacking. "I'm starved."

The relief on her mother's face told Kia that she'd done the right thing, made the right move. Kia had had the unfortunate experience of being present for rounds before. The King Doctor—almost always a man—would ask one of the Baby Docs (or Ducks as Kia thought of them; they really were like a flock—quack quack quack) to state the presenting symptoms. They'd launch into every possible scenario—all of them worst case as far as Kia was concerned—every torturous implication, horrible possibility, devastating course of treatment and its consequences, without any indication of being aware that not only were they rattling off gruesome details across her mother's weakened body but also doing so in front of her freaking-out daughter. Sometimes they'd remember to ask her to leave, but not so much anymore.

They were always in such a hurry. Sometimes Kia could barely get out before they started in. *What's the rush?* Kia wanted to ask. *The people lying in these beds aren't going anywhere.* Then Kia realized—maybe the urgency was the fear that a patient could die before the Baby Docs finished their homework. How would that affect the grade curve?

"Are you coming back?" her mother whispered from the bed.

"Yeah, of course. Just a lunch break." Kia hated the pleading look in her mom's eyes that she didn't have the strength to cover. "I'd offer to bring you back something, but that seems like cruel and unusual punishment."

Mom smiled a half-smile and Kia booked out of the room as King Doc said, "And now . . ."

Four more hours, Kia told herself as she headed down the corridor to the elevator. *You skipped yesterday,* she thought, *it's the least you can do.*

She skidded to a stop at the elevator banks. A little kid, probably about eight years old, sat in a wheelchair, an IV pole being handled by his mother, who seemed to be expending inordinate amounts of energy keeping it together. Kia spun around and took the stairs, the clomping sound of her heavy boots echoing in the empty stairwell.

She pushed through the door at basement level where the

cafeteria was and found herself face-to-face with a bulletin board crowded with notices. "*Da Vinci Code* Reading Club Meeting Wed. in the 3rd Floor Lounge," "Piano Recital on Fridays at 4 p.m.—Reserve Now!" "Storytime Ages 4–8," library hours, religious services, lectures, classes, notice after notice after notice announcing activities and events. There were ATM and stamp machines in the lobby leading into the cafeteria. Fast-food franchises, vending machines, fresh sushi, meat grilled in front of you. Kia picked up a brown plastic tray and stood in front of the dessert station, staring stupidly at a chocolate cake surrounded by cups of Jell-O.

You never had to leave this building, Kia realized. The hospital was a self-contained world. She swallowed, her throat dry. An alternate world to which she and her mother had valid passports.

"You taking the last piece?" a voice behind Kia asked.

Startled, Kia took a step away from the dessert case and whipped her head around. A short girl with beaded braids and very dark skin stood in front of her. She looked about Kia's age, with a similar sense of style: black leather jacket over black vest over black leggings with a black skirt that only barely covered her butt. Her (black) boots had pointy toes, and she wore five silver star-shaped earrings in the ear that Kia could see. The other was covered by braids.

"What?" Kia asked.

The girl's enormous almond-shaped eyes focused on Kia's nose stud. "Excellent turquoise. Like the setting."

"Thanks," Kia said. "Same on your stars."

"So are you? Taking the last piece of cake?" the girl asked. "If not, I got it. Nothing else too edible in this place."

Kia stepped aside. "All yours. It was the Jell-O that held my fascination."

The girl shook her head. "I don't see how that can qualify as food. It's made from horses' hooves or something."

"Really?"

The girl shrugged. "That's what I heard. But how can something so jiggly come from something as solid as a horse's hoof?" She grinned. "Modern science. Of course, we're at the epicenter of modern science," she added, scanning the cafeteria. "Or so all the white-coated freaks would want you to think."

"Yeah." Kia looked down at her empty tray. She could feel the girl's doe eyes on her a moment. Then the girl reached past Kia into the dessert case and pulled out the cake.

"I'm calling myself Hecate these days," the girl said. She placed the cake in the center of her tray. "My mom says it's a phase."

"What was it before?" Kia asked, somehow finding herself following the black-clad sprite to the coffee kiosk.

Hecate shot her a grin. "If I told you that, I'd have to kill you. Let's just say Mom was in her own phase when I was born."

Kia laughed and poured herself coffee from the thermos at the kiosk. It had a Starbucks logo on it. Just like the outside world. She shot half-and-half into her cup and decided coffee was all she could handle right now.

"Hospital shit does a number on the appetite, doesn't it?" Hecate asked, leading Kia to the cashier. "All I ever want is cake. I think it's the lighting in here. The lack of daylight. Oh yeah, not to mention the trauma and emotional stress. And the lovely views."

Kia looked around at the pale faces made gray in the fluorescent lighting. The IV poles. The doctors checking their beeping pagers. The tear-stained family members holding hands. The animated conversations of hospital personnel and the hyper quality of everyone else who wasn't either crying or staring into space.

"At least we don't have to make reservations," Kia said. "And there's no dress code."

"And it *is* an exclusive club," Hecate said. "True, no velvet ropes, but admittance by membership only. Oh, lucky us."

Kia smiled at Hecate. "I—I think I'm actually hungry," she said. "Save me a seat."

She went and ordered a minestrone from the soup station and made herself a salad. When she got back to the table, Hecate had already devoured the cake and was pouring sugar into her coffee.

Kia slid into the seat and dug into her salad with a plastic fork. She felt Hecate's eyes studying her.

"You ever go to Twilight Hours?" Hecate asked.

Kia shook her head. "Is that a store?"

"A club night. Wednesdays. At a place on Eighteenth Street."

"Oh. I'm not twenty-one."

"Really?" Hecate shrugged and grinned. "Me either. Well, that's what fake IDs are for. And some places let you in if you're eighteen and just don't give you drink tickets. They spin some seriously good discs. Goth, dark wave. No cover. Mixed crowd."

"Sounds fun." Kia didn't add that she wasn't eighteen either. Seventeen was close enough, right?

"You should check it out sometime. I thought maybe I'd seen you there, but I think it might have been from here. You've been coming here long?" Suddenly her eyes widened and Hecate snorted. "Wait. Sorry." She gasped, trying to stop herself from laughing. "That sounds like a pickup line. Hey, baby, come here often? Like, Cancerville is such an excellent place to hook up."

"They seem to have everything else here; why not a singles scene?" Kia suggested, grinning at Hecate.

"Stop," Hecate ordered, still laughing. "My mind is going in all the wrong places."

Kia giggled. "So, why are you here?" she asked. "Or, I guess, who . . ."

Hecate took a swig of her coffee. "Grandfather. Prostate cancer. He's really cool. My dad left around the time my little brother died, so my mom and I moved into Gramps's place."

Kia nodded. She took a few spoonfuls of soup to cover the silence.

"You?" Hecate asked.

"My mother." She took another spoonful of soup before pushing it away, suddenly aware of its canned, institutional flavor.

"My brother was real little when he died," Hecate said. "A long time ago. But it changed everything forever. The way things do, you know?"

"I do know," Kia said. She took a swig of water. "I had to move in with my dad. I had gotten used to the divorce and to hardly seeing him and now he's the parental unit again. All of it."

"Parents get weird when serious shit happens," Hecate said. "They're so unpredictable." She held her coffee cup at an odd angle, as if she wasn't aware she was holding it anymore. Her voice was a little far away. "When something happens in your family, it sucks you out of your own life, like you've disappeared into a black hole or something. And it isn't even your own crap that puts you there."

Kia nodded. "That's exactly how I've been feeling."

She wanted to ask Hecate what her brother died of and if her gramps was supposed to get better but didn't know how. Especially since it didn't seem fair to ask but not tell herself. So instead she said, "Are you in school?"

"Not this year. I'm working to save enough for college." She stood up. "You done? I want to pop outside for a smoke."

Kia swigged her now-tepid coffee and stood up. They tossed their trash and placed the trays on the counter. For a small person, Hecate covered ground quickly, so that even with her much-longer legs Kia had to work to keep up with her. Hecate also seemed to know the ins and outs of the exits, making Kia wonder how long she had been coming to the hospital or if she had simply explored more territory than Kia had.

They came out a side door and leaned against the wall. Hecate pulled a pack of cigarettes and a lighter from her bag and lit up. She shut her eyes as she took a long, deep inhale. Kia watched the trail of smoke break apart in the cooling air.

Hecate opened her eyes. She held up the cigarette. "You want one?" she asked.

Kia shook her head.

"I guess I should quit," Hecate said, looking at the cigarette. "But so far I haven't figured out a good enough reason."

She took another drag and then tipped her head toward the three white-coated women huddled together smoking near the edge of the building.

"Check that out," she said. "Gotta love the irony. They work with cancer patients all day long and still smoke. Talk about living life on the edge."

"Or having a death wish," Kia said, and immediately wanted to smack herself or take back her words.

Hecate shrugged. "Either way, you can't say they're not making an informed choice."

"And it *is* their choice," Kia said. Ugh. Now she sounded all PC or something. *Shut up now.*

Hecate checked her watch. "I've got to go. I have to get to work."

"Where do you work?" Kia asked.

"NightTimes, over on St. Marks," Hecate said. "You should come by. I'm there most days."

"Okay," Kia said, glad that Hecate seemed interested in making friends with her.

Hecate dropped her cigarette to the pavement and ground it out with the pointy toe of her boot. Then she rummaged in her bag and pulled out a dark blue postcard, which she held out to Kia.

Kia took the card. It showed a picture of a woman in vaguely medieval dress, with long flowing hair. Very Pre-Raphaelite. The woman had a dreamy expression on her face. Behind her, a striking man held her hair away from her neck and looked as if he were about to bite her. Ornate black letters said Darkness Reigns Every Sunday Night across the top. On the bottom was an address.

"What's this?" Kia asked.

"Vampire night in Brooklyn," Hecate said. "It's fun. Awesome DJ, only five bucks cover." She cocked her head at Kia and smiled conspiratorially. "And they don't check IDs too carefully. I'll be there after I get off work. Things don't really get started until around eleven anyway."

Kia was going to ask what a "vampire night" was but after the cigarette thing decided that the best thing to do would be to nod and smile. "Thanks." She slipped the flyer into her boot.

Hecate readjusted the strap of her bag on her shoulder. "Sometimes it's good to get dressed up, go to the club, not think about hospitals or parents or work or anything. Just get lost in the music. The dancing. If you're into dancing."

Kia thought back to the previous night, the Wiccan circle and how she felt while she was spinning and twirling. "If I have a choice between thinking and dancing," Kia said, "I'll pick dancing every time."

"You going back in?" Hecate asked. "I've got to say bye to Gramps and then take off."

"Oh, right." Kia looked up at the building. She had vowed to spend at least four hours here today; she'd barely made it through two. "I'm going to check out the gift shop first." They went around to the main entrance.

"So maybe I'll see you around," Hecate said before heading off to the elevators.

Kia scoured the gift shop for something to read to her mom. The romance novels and thrillers weren't going to interest her. Kia finally settled on a book on politics that came down hard on all of her mom's list of "usual suspects." Her mother enjoyed political rants, so Kia thought it would be a good distraction, and it looked pretty funny, too.

She felt less apprehensive as she walked out of the elevator on her mom's floor. It helped that she had a game plan—this book would take a while to read.

She came around the curtain and stopped when she saw her mom's closed eyes and slow, deep breaths. She was asleep.

Did it count as a visit if her mother spent the rest of the afternoon sleeping?

A chunky nurse came in to check her mom's readings. She must have jostled something because Kia's mom startled awake. Her eyes looked misty and out of focus.

"Your daughter's here," the nurse said in a clipped Asian accent.

Her mother looked confused and then slowly turned her head toward Kia, who was still standing at the foot of the bed.

"Who's there?" Kia's mom asked. Her voice sounded hollow and echoey. "I can see you."

"Mom?" Kia said.

"Mom?" Kia's mother repeated. She shut her eyes and swallowed. "Swimming."

"What?" Kia asked, her throat tight.

"I feel as if I'm swimming." She opened her eyes. They were a little more focused now. "Hello, honey . . ." Her voice trailed off.

The nurse finished what she was doing and patted Kia's mom on the shoulder. "You rest now."

As she passed Kia, the nurse said, "She's just had a sedative for pain. She'll be in and out for several hours."

"Oh."

"Honey," Kia's mom said.

Kia took a step closer to the bed. She wondered what kind of pain the medication was for. Where did it hurt? Should she be careful and not sit on the bed anymore?

"Honey," her mom repeated. Only this time it sounded as if she were just trying out the word without really knowing what it meant.

"Yes, Mom?"

"What?"

"Do you need something?"

Her mother shook her head.

"Do you—do you want me to let you rest?" Kia's heart thudded a little. She hoped her mom would say yes and she could leave, but then felt terrible about having the thought.

Her mother nodded. "Yes, rest. You rest."

Kia bit her lip. "I don't need to rest, Mom, you do."

"Yes, rest."

Kia stood there, uncertain. Her mom was clearly elsewhere. "Okay, Mom," Kia said, putting the book down on the nightstand. "I'll come by again tomorrow. I got you a book."

"That's good."

The lines in her mom's face smoothed as she sank into sleep. Before Kia had even left the room, her mother's breathing was deep and slow.

Kia quickly walked the ten blocks home. As she neared the apartment building, she slowed down, realizing there was no point in hurrying. It wasn't as if she had anything to do. Carol had a music rehearsal and then planned to do some serious making out with the cello player. Aaron was trapped watching his baby sister, Miranda, aka The Surprise.

The doorman and Kia played their usual "Kia is invisible"

game and ignored each other as she stepped through the glass doors into the plush lobby. Riding up, she tried to think of a way to occupy her time.

She unlocked the door and shouted, "I'm home," just in case her dad was naked or with someone or something. The first week she moved in, both things had happened—luckily not at the same time.

"I'm home too," her dad answered from the living room. Kia could hear a sports event droning in the background.

She passed the living room and saw her dad sitting in sweats on the leather sofa, wearing his reading glasses and surrounded by piles of files. He glanced up and noticed her standing at the edge of the room. He swapped glasses to look at her. "So how was your mom?"

Since the divorce her dad had stopped saying "Mom" as if it was her name and had switched to "*your* mom," as if he had no relation to the woman whatsoever.

"Did you have a good visit?" he asked.

"Not so hot," Kia said, in response to both questions.

"Oh." He looked at her for a minute as if waiting for her to continue. She didn't. He cleared his throat, and it looked to Kia as if he was bracing himself, prepping for some task. "Did . . . did something happen?"

Kia looked down at her fingernails. It was definitely time to reapply the polish—it was all chipped. *That's what I can do tonight.*

"Kia?"

She looked up. "No, nothing unusual. Same old. You know, hospital shit."

"Kia," he said in a warning tone, "language." He didn't like her to swear. He claimed it wasn't a moral issue or even a question of manners issue but aesthetics. "Cursing is a lazy form of speech," he'd say.

"I mean, hospital *stuff*."

He rolled his eyes. "Not a big improvement, but I'll accept it for now." He straightened a folder on the glass table in front of him. "I've got a load of work to do," he said. "I'm starving. Let's just order in, okay? Pick what you want, and order me the Buddhist Delight."

Kia smirked. "It's only four," she pointed out. "Didn't you notice all the daylight?"

Her dad's attention went to the large window. "Oh, right. I guess I forgot to eat lunch. Well, I'll grab something now and when you get hungry, order. I can always microwave the Buddhist Delight later."

He pushed aside the folders, stood, and stretched. "This case is going to kill me." He walked past Kia and into the kitchen. Kia went into her room and shut the door.

She sat on her bed for a few minutes, then lay on her back for a little while longer. Her brain felt empty, as if she couldn't think of anything to think about. Rolling over, she grabbed the remote on the bedside table and clicked on the TV. Nothing held her attention. She shut it off.

Lying flat on her bed again, one arm under her head, she stared at the smooth cream-colored ceiling and sensed the blood in her veins. She shifted position—the awareness was still there. Not good.

She got up and flipped through her CDs. Nothing drew her.

As she pulled her books out of her backpack, a CD fell out. The one that Virgil had given her.

That asshole. She skidded the jewel case across the floor, where it careened like a hockey puck until it stopped under her bed.

This time she shut her eyes and grabbed a CD from her stack. Opening her eyes again, she saw she had chosen Random's latest.

"Appropriate," she murmured. She dropped the CD into the player and turned it on high.

The thumping bass and the insistent drums matched the sensation of the throbbing just under Kia's skin. She turned the volume up even higher, hoping to drown out the sound inside her with the crashing synthetic pulsing noise. She stood in the center of her temporary room and thudded a foot, getting the beat into her legs, letting it crawl up her body, wanting it to push out the need running the length of her arms. She threw back her head, raised her arms, and started to dance.

"You gave me the wrong idea," she shouted along with the singer. "You made me think there was hope!" She danced hard, danced like a maniac, like a stripper, like a TV star, like a guy, like a Wiccan; she danced like Aaron, then Carol. She danced like she was never going to stop, never had to. She could feel her heart racing. It was working. She could dance it out, banish it; she didn't have to turn to cutting.

A pounding on the door. "Kia!" her dad shouted. "Turn that music down."

She flung her head side to side, thrusting her shoulders forward, then back, her spine rippling. "You gave me the way in, the way out!" she sang.

"Kia!"

She turned her back to the door, too much competition, too many sounds, from the speakers, from beyond the door, from inside her.

"Kia! I mean it."

Kia kept singing. "But now I—"

The door opened, her father walked in, and suddenly the only sound was Kia screeching, "Know I was a dope."

"Kia," her dad said. "Jesus. The walls are shaking."

Kia stared at him. She couldn't hear him; her veins were screaming.

He gave her a sheepish grin. "I get it. I played my music loud too. But crank it down to a reasonable level. I'm trying to work."

Kia gave her head a little shake. "Right. Sorry."

"So we're good here, right?" he asked.

"Yeah, sure."

"Good." He left the room, shutting the door behind him.

Kia spun on her clunky heel, walked into the bathroom, and pulled out a razor.

FOUR

Stop laughing!" Aaron ordered the next night, only it didn't carry much weight since he was giggling. The sight of him in a turquoise kimono made for someone five inches shorter was really hard to take seriously. Kia and Carol fell laughing against each other, then onto the floor. They barely escaped landing on the pizza box with the remains of their dinner still in it.

"Where did you get that monstrosity?" Kia gasped, trying to stop laughing long enough to ask the question.

"From the Drama Department," Aaron said, striking a model's hand-on-hip-head-thrown-back pose.

"From last semester's *Mikado*," Carol added, rummaging through the leftover crusts in the pizza box.

"I take it your costume has something to do with tonight's festivities," Kia said, crunching on pizza crust.

"I got them for you too," he said. He pulled two more

kimonos out of his duffel bag and tossed them to Carol and Kia.

"No way!" Carol said, pulling the satin robe off her head, where it had landed. "I am not wearing this."

"Me either," Kia chimed. She held the pink robe up to her long-sleeved black turtleneck. "Did you really think this was me?"

"Come on, guys," Aaron wheedled. "We need ceremonial robes to perform our first official coven ceremony."

Kia gaped at him. "Our what?"

"I decided after that ceremony in the park that we are going to become witches," Aaron said. "Cast spells. Do rituals."

Kia burst out laughing. "You are deeply, deeply twisted."

"That's why you love me," Aaron countered.

Carol shook her head, then grinned. "Okay, I'm game. But no pictures! Come on, Kia." She stood and headed toward the bathrobe.

Kia stood up, then stopped, her smile frozen on her face. The sleeves would only come down to her elbows.

Aaron knelt down and started pulling some bags from his duffel. "Candles. Herbs." He glanced around the room. "Kia, can you go grab some matches from the kitchen? Oh, and some salt."

"Okay." Kia dropped the robe on Aaron's rumpled bed and went into the cramped kitchen. Baby paraphernalia was everywhere, so she had to be careful not to step on some toy or knock over the bottles, pacifiers, and baby food jars as she rummaged in the cupboard for a box of matches. Aaron's parents had taken The Surprise to meet some of their old hippie friends who also had a baby afterthought.

She took the saltshaker and matches back into Aaron's room. It had once been a fairly spacious bedroom, but since the arrival of The Surprise, a wall had been built down the center to turn it into two extremely small rooms. Carol and Aaron, both wearing kimonos now, put candles in different spots around the cramped room.

"Here you go," Kia said, putting the matches and saltshaker on Aaron's dresser.

Aaron consulted a thick book with a spooky cover. "Oh, we need a bowl of water too. And something to represent air."

"Like what?" Carol asked, sticking a bright yellow candle into a holder.

Aaron studied the book again. "A feather. Chimes. A fan." He scanned the room, then snapped his fingers. "Got it!" He dashed out and came back holding a little battery-operated personal fan. "My mom was always hot those last months she was pregnant."

He placed the fan carefully and stepped back, admiring the setup. He looked up at Kia and Carol and announced, "We are ready to begin. Oh, once Kia changes."

Kia quickly slipped the kimono on over her clothes. "This is fine. Let's not waste any more time."

Aaron looked disappointed but was obviously eager to get started. He piled some books in the middle of the tiny room. "Okay. These books say to cast a circle. Then it's time for some serious chanting and dancing. Now, do what I tell you and follow me when I start walking around in a circle," Aaron instructed.

Kia saluted. "Yes, sir."

Aaron took Carol and Kia's hands. "Shut your eyes and breathe, slowly and deeply."

Kia closed her eyes and felt Carol's small cool hand and Aaron's large, warmer one. She tried to do what Aaron said, but her brain just kept spinning. *I can't believe I slipped again,* she thought. *So soon.*

"Let all the tensions and worries of the day drain out of you," Aaron crooned.

Yeah, right, Kia thought, but she ordered herself to pay attention to Aaron.

"Feel your breath," Aaron said. "In and out again."

After a few moments, she realized that she and her friends were all breathing together. It felt cozy, as if they were sharing a soft blanket. They released hands and Aaron used the baton to make a pentagram in the air.

Aaron crossed to the little propeller fan and picked it up. Holding the fan out in front of him, he intoned, "Hail to the element of air. Come join us in our circle tonight, giving us your strength and your protection."

He flicked the switch on the battery-operated fan and Kia felt its breeze as he held it first in front of himself, then in front of Carol, then in front of Kia. "We are your children, air. We welcome you."

He turned off the fan and placed it back on the floor. He moved in a circular path to the red candle. He lit it and held it in front of him just as he did with the fan. "Hail to the element of fire. Come join us in our circle tonight, giving us your strength and your protection." He passed his hand just above the flame, then held it in front of Carol. He nodded at her, and she passed her hand above the flame. Then he did the same with Kia.

Aaron's good at this, Kia thought as the heat from the flame made her hand glow.

"We are your children, fire," Aaron said. "We welcome you." He placed the candle back on the floor.

Now he moved around the circle to the bowl of water. "Hail to the element of water. Come join us in our circle tonight, giving us your strength and your protection." He stuck a finger into the water and dabbed his forehead with it. Then he had Carol and Kia do the same thing.

Kia found the repetition soothing. She felt herself relaxing.

He had arrived at the saltshaker. "Hail to the element of earth." He shook some salt into his hand and licked it. Carol and Kia repeated his action, then he returned to his original spot and said, "Our circle is cast."

Aaron, Kia, and Carol all looked at each other. *Now what?* Kia wondered.

Aaron gestured for them to sit. "There's a list in one of these books about what kind of magic works best on Sundays."

Carol held up one of Aaron's books. "It says here that Sunday is a good day for spells of protection, strength, and healing." Carol looked at Kia. "I think we should do a healing spell."

Kia swallowed hard before she spoke. "I—I don't know. . . ."

"Great idea," Aaron said, flipping pages. "Okay, this is a general healing spell, and we can just adjust it so that it works for Kia's mom."

Carol knelt beside Aaron and peered at the book. "Do we have what we need?"

"Let's see. We've got the blue candles. We also need to drink water. I guess we can just drink from the water bowl."

Carol snorted. "That makes us sound like dogs."

"Woof," Aaron said.

Carol handed the book to Kia. "Here, you can say the words," she offered. Kia's heart thudded and she stared at the page, the words blurry in the flickering candlelight.

"I—I don't think I can," she finally admitted, letting the book fall shut. She could feel Carol and Aaron look at each other.

"I'll do it if you want," Carol offered.

"But wouldn't my mother have to be the one to do the spell anyway?" Kia asked. "Since we're supposed to drink in healing powers."

"I think it can be done for anyone, by anyone," Aaron said. "Let Carol try."

Kia shrugged and said, "If you want."

Carol took the book. "Why don't you light the candle?"

Kia complied, relieved her hand didn't shake as she held out the match.

"Okay. I call upon the powers of the elements to aid me in this healing spell. I am asking for help in healing Kia's mom."

Kia studied her shoelaces.

"I ask that air blow away her cancer."

Kia felt her stomach tighten.

"I ask that fire transform sickness into health."

Kia swallowed.

"I ask that water wash away the bad cells."

Kia shut her eyes.

"I ask that earth ground me and help to manifest my wishes on this material plane."

Kia opened her eyes again and stared at the candle flames.

Carol picked up the water bowl. Her brow furrowed. "Should I drink this or should Kia?"

"All three of us," Aaron said. "That way it's a wish from all of us."

"We drink in the power of water to heal," Carol declared. She took a sip and then passed the bowl to Kia. Kia's hands trembled and she sloshed a bit of water out of the bowl. She sipped quickly and handed the bowl to Aaron. Aaron took a drink and placed the bowl back in its place. "Let's say the last words all together," he said.

"As I will it, so it will be!" Carol, Kia, and Aaron said in unison.

"Now we have to raise energy and send the spell out to the universe," Aaron said, getting to his feet.

"How?" Kia asked.

"Chanting. Dancing. Like we did in the park."

"What should we chant?" Carol asked.

Aaron smiled. "How's this? As I will it, so it will be. As I will it, so it will be."

As Aaron continued to chant, Kia and Carol joined in. Over and over, they repeated the words, adding clapping and stomping. Then Aaron led them in a circle around his tiny room, stepping up onto his bed and coming back down the other side.

Around and around Kia went, clapping, shouting. Stomping her feet hard. Jumping down from Aaron's bed. Carol twirled in front of her, and Aaron jumped up and down behind her, and all the time they inscribed a circle on the floor of the room, chanting, "As I will it, so it will be."

Without even a signal to each other, they each suddenly stopped circling and started dancing in place. Kia grew warm with the movement; the whole room seemed to have risen in temperature.

Shooting their arms straight up into the air, they cried, "As I will it, so it will be!" and abruptly stopped. They stood there, the only sound their labored breathing, mixed with tiny soft laughs.

"Wow," Aaron said finally.

"I'd say that was some serious energy raising," Carol said.

Kia nodded. "Definitely electric." She could feel her heart racing, her body alive and vibrating.

"So are we finished?" Carol asked.

"We have to close the circle," Aaron said. "Just say thanks to all the elements and blow out the candles."

Once they had undone the ceremony, Aaron had them all take hands again. "The circle is open but unbroken. We shall all meet again."

"We do all hang out together all the time," Kia said.

"But it's nice to acknowledge it formally," Aaron replied. He flopped onto his bed. "So that was pretty cool."

"Wouldn't it be great if it could really work?" Carol said. She settled on the floor in front of Aaron's closet.

Kia leaned on the windowsill, tapping a foot. There was still a lot of energy running through her, energy that reminded her of the previous night in her room. "So now what do you guys want to do?"

"It's already after ten. What is there to do?" Aaron asked. "On a Sunday."

Good point. Then Kia remembered. Sunday. That was the

vampire night. The one Hecate had told her about. She rummaged through her backpack and found the crumpled flyer. "We could go to this. It's supposed to be fun."

Aaron took the postcard from her. "Vampires?"

"It's in Brooklyn," Carol said, peering over Aaron's shoulder.

"The girl who gave it to me seemed cool," Kia said. "Hey, we went to your witch thing. Now we should check out a vampire thing."

"What, some Buffy wannabes?" Carol asked.

"Technically, if they're vampires," Aaron pointed out, "Buffy is their worst nightmare."

"Spike is hot. So is Angel," Kia said, knowing Aaron's weakness.

"You have a point. It could be okay."

"Tell your mom that you're going to keep me company at my house," Kia told Carol. "Just say my dad's out of town or something." She turned to Aaron. "You could leave your parents a note and tell them the same thing."

"Sounds like a plan to me," Aaron said.

FIVE

A long subway journey later, they were in the Williamsburg section of Brooklyn. They emerged aboveground on a busy street filled with coffee shops, restaurants, clothing stores, and pedestrians—mostly young and hip. As they followed the directions on the flyer, the heavily trafficked streets gave way to wider, more deserted ones, and the stores vanished, replaced by mysterious industrial buildings with blacked-out windows.

"Are you sure we're going the right way?" Carol asked, stepping over some broken glass.

Kia squinted at the flyer. "According to this, the club should be on the next street."

"If it's not there," Aaron said nervously, "we're turning around and going back. This is no-man's-land."

Kia saw some smokers puffing away in a huddle of leather jackets up the street. A small red light above a doorway indicated an entrance. "I bet that's it," she said, darting ahead. She wanted to see Hecate again. Wanted to stay out late and not get home till sunrise.

She wanted to keep vampire hours.

A large man wearing a long black cloak over leather pants and a high-collared white shirt with a ruffled front stood at the doorway. That was when Kia remembered—none of them had ID.

She held up the flyer as she approached the door. The door dude glanced at her, at the flyer, and grinned.

Fangs. The guy had fangs! Recovering quickly, Kia grinned back.

"They're with me," she added, tipping her head toward Aaron and Carol. Aaron was openly staring at the man's mouth, and Carol was looking down at the ground. She looked as if she were trying not to laugh.

The guy narrowed his eyes at Carol and Aaron suspiciously, then at Kia. Kia gave him an imploring look. "Newbies," she said, hoping that would cover whatever offense Carol and Aaron were committing.

The guy smirked and nodded, as if he and Kia were sharing an inside joke. "Go ahead." He stood away from the door.

They walked into a party scene in full throttle. The first thing Kia noticed was the bass line and drumbeat thumping into her heart. One of her favorite songs was blasting from the nearby loudspeakers. The room was crowded despite the cavernous proportions of the space. She, Carol, and Aaron were instantly separated by the flow of people making their way on and off the dance floor, to and from the bar, in and out the door. Kia pressed forward.

The enormous room was illuminated by flickering candles in sconces along the walls and hanging overhead in chandeliers. Lights aimed at the walls cast eerie pools of red on the rough surfaces. In the erratic, dim light, and because almost everyone in the room was wearing black, the mass of dancing bodies blurred into each other. Kia stood at the outskirts of the dancing, feeling its pull, wanting to blur into the mass too.

A hand tugged her jacket. "Wait up," Carol said.

"What do you think they call this look?" Aaron asked. "High dungeon?"

"Faux torture chamber?" Carol suggested. "Yeah, like *that's* appealing."

Kia suddenly had the uncanny sense that someone was watching her. Slowly she turned and gazed up at the DJ booth above the bar. A pale face framed by pale hair peered down at the crowd between rough iron bars. Peered down at Kia.

Those are intense eyes, she thought. *Black, almost.*

He vanished, and the music changed. The beat revved up again.

"Right, Kia?" Carol was saying.

"What?" Kia asked.

"We should move out of the way," Carol said. "Out of the path of the door."

"Oh, right."

They wove their way through the black-clad throngs. Both men and women smiled at her as she moved around them, often revealing fangs. Kia found herself smiling back.

They all seemed so friendly. Kia felt . . . *welcome.*

Aaron hustled them into a little alcove, where they piled

onto a burgundy velvet love seat. He stretched out his legs and rested his sneakered feet on the small table.

"Did you see those fangs?" Aaron asked, shaking his head and laughing.

"What kind of freak would do that?" Carol said, giggling. "Do you think they're permanent?"

"Check out that dude," Aaron said, nodding toward the end of the bar. A man wearing a Victorian brocade jacket over a vest and silk pants stood holding a glass of red wine. A woman in a corset and long skirt approached him. They spoke a minute, then he grabbed her long hair, yanked back her head, and bent over her throat.

"Is he biting her?" Carol asked, nearly squeaking.

Aaron snorted. "Man, she's going to have a major hickey in the morning."

A crowd gathered around the pair at the bar, urging them on, and then another man bit the woman on the other side of her neck. His hands slid down her long skirt, slowly, then up again while the other man rested his hand on the exposed part of her breast above the top of the low-cut corset.

How intense is this going to get? Kia wondered, her eyes glued on the scene even as she felt a blush tingle her cheeks.

The woman's body seemed to go limp. The two "vampires" biting her held her up, pressing her against the bar. Kia's own knees felt weak as she watched the woman clutch at the two men's arms. There was a desperation in the way she gripped them, as if she needed to pull the men closer.

Watching that woman giving over completely, letting physical sensation inhabit her entire body, Kia felt warm all over. She forced herself to ignore Aaron and Carol making jokes beside her, talking about outfits and how lame the scene was, timing the biting, taking bets on how long it would go.

Then the first man, the one in the brocade jacket, pushed the other man aside and, in one sudden movement, lifted the swooning woman into his arms and carried her away through the approving crowd.

The spurned second man slowly wiped his mouth, bared his fangs at the crowd in a grimace, and stalked off in the opposite direction.

Wow, Kia thought, too stunned to process.

There was a crackle from the loudspeakers. "Welcome, all, to the gathering of the undead," a voice said.

Kia looked around and noticed that there was now someone standing on the stage.

He spoke again into the microphone. "I see familiar faces. I see new faces. But what I see most of all is our fierce, predatory power. We are vampire. We embrace the darkness, and without the Mundane's fear of death, we have no fear at all."

"We are vampire!" a group shouted near the stage.

"We are sustained by blood. Blood is life, so we feed on it," the man on the stage crooned. "We eat life, we breathe life, we who have gone beyond life. It is our blood right."

"Our blood right!" someone shouted.

"The dark is our home. We are part of the eternal, and that is our power."

Kia's eyes traveled from the man at the microphone to the skulls that lined the front of the stage. The symbols for infinity that decorated the black velvet curtain. The goblets filled with dark red liquid on pedestals behind the man. She shivered but not from cold, not from fear.

"Embrace your dark selves," the man said. "Do not fear your shadow side. Embrace it, for it will empower you."

Kia felt herself nodding. Could she embrace her dark side? Could she accept the part of herself that needed to cut her skin, release her blood, strike at her own flesh? Maybe it wasn't so terrible after all?

Kia glanced at Carol. She looked bored and slightly disgusted. Aaron just seemed amused, and it made Kia's shoulders tense. She didn't want to hear what either of them might say.

The man on the stage lifted a taloned hand. His nails were long and curved and sharpened to little points. "Now let's turn the night back over to Damon, our illustrious DJ. And dance till the sun extinguishes our revels."

The crowd applauded, a few people howled like werewolves, and music blasted again from the loudspeakers.

"That was so—" Aaron began.

Kia cut him off. "I want to dance," she said "I love this song."

She headed for the dance floor, not really caring if they followed or not. She wanted to burrow more deeply into this strange new place. Dancing seemed the best route in.

All around her, people surged with the pulsating beat. Kia let herself get lost in the sound, in the rhythm. She shut her eyes to feel it more intensely, to let it surround her. Surrounded by darkness and somehow feeling light.

Someone banged into her and she found herself staring up into red eyes. The gaunt face smiled down at her, his fangs small and discreet. "Excuse me," he said.

Kia smiled back and let him wriggle by. Carol stared after him. Kia hadn't noticed until then that Carol and Aaron were dancing beside her.

"What a weirdo," Carol said. "I can't believe he's actually wearing fangs."

Kia started dancing again. She liked that the guy was extreme, was doing the vampire thing totally. He looked real— and wasn't that the point? To get dressed up and create a whole alternate world?

Kia wished she had done more to get ready and noticed that Aaron and Carol were getting the same suspicious looks on the dance floor that they had gotten outside. Here it was Kia who fit in.

Scanning the crowd, she wondered if this was a secret world for most of these people. An entirely alternate life.

A vault, Kia thought, looking up at the arched stone entryways. That's what Vampyre Central reminded her of—a place to hold and keep secrets safe. The kind of place where Kia could have as many secrets as she wanted and no one would be disappointed in her.

"You came!"

Kia turned and saw Hecate coming toward her through the crowd. She was dressed even more provocatively than she had been at the hospital, in a plastic micro-mini and a vinyl corset.

"So what do you think?" Hecate asked Kia.

"The music rocks," Kia said.

"Yeah, Damon's awesome," Hecate said. She glanced toward the DJ booth. "Not to mention hot."

Kia felt Carol and Aaron standing there, just standing. They had stopped dancing and were waiting to be introduced. For the first time ever, Kia felt uncomfortable about claiming their friendship.

"Carol, Aaron, this is Hecate," Kia said.

"So I'm guessing this is kind of new for you," Hecate said to Carol.

"Uh, yeah." Ordinarily Carol behaved as if she were the hostess of the universe. But with Hecate she kept quiet.

"So are you a *vampire*?" Aaron asked. He drew out the word *vampire* and said it with a bad Transylvanian accent. Kia cringed.

Hecate ignored the question and smirked. "What were you thinking?" She gestured at Carol and Aaron's clothing. "I'm surprised Scream let you in."

"Scream?" Carol said, raising an eyebrow. "Someone calls himself Scream?"

"I'm going to get a drink," Hecate said. "You want anything?"

"Definitely," Kia said.

They wove their way to the long bar. Hecate ordered the round since she was the one with the ID. Kia noticed there were a few kids probably around her age, but mostly the crowd was in their twenties, and some a little older.

Red confetti drifted down onto the bar in front of her. She looked up and once again stared into black eyes. The DJ grinned down at her from his booth above the bar. He was leaning on the rusty-looking iron railing, his fair hair feathering around his pale face.

He looks like a drawing. The high cheekbones, the smooth plane of his forehead, the short, sharp nose, the curve of his lips all created shadows and surfaces perfectly laid out for charcoal. And slightly unreal. From this distance, Kia couldn't tell if he had fangs or not, but if he did, Kia was sure they'd look good on him.

"Damon's sizzling hot, don't you think?" Hecate said, nudging Kia in the side with her elbow. Kia flushed and looked down at her drink. It was a muddy red and served in a martini glass.

"What is this?" she asked, grateful to have an escape from the DJ's intense eyes.

"Bloodbath," Hecate said, lifting her glass. "Cheers!" She clinked Kia's drink and took a sip.

"What's in it?" Aaron asked, eyeing the drink suspiciously.

"Red wine and Chambord," Hecate said, licking her purple-outlined lips. "What—did you think it was the blood of virgins or something?"

"Nah," Aaron said. He picked up the martini glass, spilling a little as he brought it to his mouth. "I don't think you'd find any of those here."

Hecate laughed. "You got that right."

Carol held back her long hair and bent over her glass. She took a dainty sip without lifting it up. She cocked her head. "Not bad," she decided.

Kia ran a finger along the stem of the glass, trying to sense if the DJ was still looking at her. She glanced up through her thick bangs. Nope, he was gone again.

She sipped the bloodbath. She was relieved to see that Carol looked a little more comfortable and had started chatting with Hecate.

Kia turned and leaned against the bar so she could watch the scene in front of her. A striking burgundy-haired woman dressed completely in white stood out in high relief against the ocean of black. She was having an earnest conversation with two extremely overweight women, both wearing skimpy leather outfits. Two men approached them, and they actually seemed just as interested in the heavy women as the thin one. Interesting. The woman in white eventually excused herself and the men and the heavy leather-clad women headed for the dance floor.

Two bare-chested men in leather pants strolled by, their bodies covered in vivid tattoos. One man's entire back was tattooed with the image of a vampire biting the neck of a naked woman. They eyed Kia and her friends, nodded at Hecate, and kept walking.

"Nipple piercing has to hurt," Aaron said as he watched the men vanish into the crowd.

A woman in a vinyl jumpsuit and a mask standing beside Aaron let out a sharp laugh. "Maybe that's the point," she said with a sly grin. "Got a problem with pain?"

"Well, actually, yes," Aaron said, taking a step closer to Carol. "I'm against it."

The woman picked up her drink—a strange green concoction—and drank it all in one gulp.

A man in his late twenties approached the woman. "Hey, Queenie, haven't seen you in a while."

"I haven't wanted to be seen," the woman responded coldly, then walked away.

The guy shrugged and slid an arm around Hecate. "Want to get happy?"

Hecate shook him off. "Not with you, thanks. They don't either," she added, indicating Kia, Carol, and Aaron.

The guy smiled, and Kia realized his eyes were out of focus. "I get that. Cool." He shambled away again.

"I don't know if you guys drop or sniff or whatever, but never get anything from that creep," Hecate said.

"It's pretty late," Carol said. "We should be getting back."

"You sure?" Hecate replied. "The party kicks into gear around now."

Kia scanned the room. It was more crowded—she hadn't thought that was possible. People had spread up onto the stage and were dancing there. The feeling in the club had become even more charged, more intense. Kia felt herself revving up with it as if she'd plugged into a special battery pack.

"Come on," Carol urged. "We have a long way to go to get home."

"Yeah, plus we're going to be useless tomorrow as it is," Aaron added.

Kia knew they were right: that subway ride wasn't going to be pretty. And there was school in the morning. "Okay," she said with a sigh. "But I need to hit the ladies' room first."

Carol shuddered. "I don't even want to think what that experience might be like. We'll wait right here."

Hecate pointed Kia toward the bathrooms and headed over to a group of kids wearing lots of metal jewelry. They looked closer to high school age. "Thanks for the invite," Kia called to Hecate. Hecate nodded and grinned and then joined the conversation.

Kia made it to the bathroom. *I don't know what Carol was so worried about,* she thought as she washed her hands in the sink. She checked herself in the mirror. Next time, she'd really do it up.

The woman in white Kia had seen earlier appeared in the doorway. "You're new," she said. Her voice was soft and low. Her burgundy hair was cut in a severe 1920s bob, like flappers wore, and the dress was an extravagant lace concoction that showed off her slim but shapely figure to full advantage. Her blue eyes were thickly outlined in black, and her lips were pale, pale pink. She looked older than Kia, somewhere in her late twenties.

She stepped into the bathroom. "I haven't seen you before."

"No," Kia said. "My first time here."

"And . . . ?" the woman asked, her voice a caress. Kia realized the woman had very subtle, very small fangs.

Why does she care what I think? Kia wondered, flattered.

"And I want to come back," Kia said.

'So you enjoy our vampire community?" the woman asked.

"Yes," Kia said. "I'm glad I came."

"Good. We welcome new nocturnal creatures," the woman said. "I am called Kali."

"Kia."

"Welcome, Kia," Kali said.

"Thanks." Kia realized Carol and Aaron were probably going to come looking for her if she didn't get back to the bar soon. She was suddenly uncomfortable about them meeting this elegant, otherworldly woman. "My friends are waiting for me," Kia apologized. "I need to go."

Kali nodded. "Of course." She reached into her tiny velvet

handbag and pulled out a small postcard. "We will see each other again."

Kia took the card and glanced at it. It was an invitation to another vampire night. This flyer said: *Private party. Admittance with this card only. Invitation not transferable.*

"Thanks," Kia said, slipping the card into her bag. "I think we will."

SIX

Monday at lunch Aaron laid his head on his arms. "Wake me up when it's time for chemistry," he said.

"I was totally useless in technique today," Carol complained, jabbing her salad with her plastic fork. "I just couldn't get my fingers to behave."

"They were napping," Aaron said, his eyes closed. "Like I want to be."

Kia yawned. She was tired too, but so what? School was just school, like it always was. But last night—that was something different.

"Do you think you can get some more costumes from the shop?" Kia asked Aaron. "Like you did with those witchy robes?"

Aaron sat back up and dusted crumbs from his cheek. "For what?" he asked.

"To wear to the vampire club," Kia said. She swigged her Diet Coke. "I don't know, corsets or Victorian-style stuff."

Carol looked at her. "You want to go back?" she asked.

"Yeah," Kia said. "I think we'll have a better time if we seriously do it up. Blend better."

"Gee. So where should I go to get those very attractive red-eyed contact lenses?" Aaron said.

"Yeah," Carol added, giggling. "Or fake fangs for freaks."

"Losers R Us," Aaron said, laughing.

Kia bristled. "I didn't think they were such freaks," she said. "I had fun."

"Maybe for checking out once," Carol said. "But it was just so . . ." She shrugged. "I mean, a whole scene pretending to be vampires? How lame is that?"

"How is that any lamer than people pretending to be witches?" Kia said. "And our little magic spells. Like that was oh so hip and real."

"Hey," Aaron said. "Wicca is an actual spiritual practice. And the spells are fun."

Carol nodded. "Yeah, even if they don't work, it's not as if anything bad could happen."

"Nothing was going to happen to us there," Kia argued.

"Hecate seemed okay, I guess," Carol said. "But the other people there? And she said it was only just getting going when we left. How weird did it get after we were gone?"

"That's something I really don't want to find out," Aaron said. "The subway at two a.m. is weird enough for me."

Kia looked away from her friends and glanced around the cafeteria. Virgil sat at a nearby table, with a couple of goth girls Kia knew a little bit from some of her classes. They basically tolerated Kia because she was Virgil's friend. She wondered if any of them had ever gone to a vampire night. Had Virgil? They hadn't spoken at all in homeroom. Kia was still pissed at him but too tired to really care. And he seemed kind of pissed off at her. Well, *he* was the jerk the other day. If anyone should apologize, it should be him.

"I have another spell I want to work on," Aaron said, changing the subject.

Kia plunked down her soda. "Do you honestly think lighting some candles and dancing around is really going to affect anything?"

"It could," Aaron said. "We just have to give it a chance. And practice. In fact, want to come over and do it again today?"

"Sure," Carol said.

"No thanks," Kia said. "I'm going to see my mom today." She tapped her heel on the floor with a quick beat, her knee bouncing up and down.

"Tell her hi," Carol said.

"And who knows," Aaron added. "Maybe our spell for her worked."

"Yeah, I'm sure we've discovered the cure for cancer," Kia said sarcastically.

Aaron cringed. "I'm just saying, maybe she'll be doing a little better. . . ."

"Yeah, we'll see," Kia muttered.

"You look as bad as I feel," Kia's mom said as Kia plopped onto the chair. "My roomie's gone. Should I book you her bed?"

"Any bed would make me happy right now," Kia said, feeling dizzy with exhaustion. "Didn't get much sleep last night."

"Hmm. As your mom, I'm torn between hoping that's because you were having fun and worried that you were having too much fun on a weeknight."

Kia laughed. "I was with Aaron and Carol," she said, telling mostly the truth.

"Okay," her mom replied. "I'm glad you're doing things with your friends and not spending all your time worrying."

Kia's brow furrowed. She suddenly realized that the entire time she had been at Vampyre Central she hadn't thought once about her mom, the hospital, her dad, nothing. She felt a flutter of guilt and then realized her mom really meant what she said: she didn't want Kia to spend her life being afraid and worried.

"Help me up," her mom said, holding her thin arms toward Kia.

"Sure." Kia helped her mother slide into a more comfortable position on the bed. "You seem better," she said.

"Yeah, not so bad today," her mother replied. She shrugged. "Don't know why, exactly."

Kia blinked.

"Same meds, same doctors, same routine, but less pain," her mother continued. "Well, don't ask why if it's going well, right?" She smiled. "Just be grateful for the little things."

"Right," Kia agreed, shifting in her chair. There was no way, though. It had to be a coincidence.

"I did enjoy having you read to me the other day," Kia's mom said. "Would you do that again?"

"Sure. Do you want to hear the newspaper or the book I bought?"

"Book," her mom declared. "Headlines these days just make me anxious."

"Okay." Kia settled onto the bed beside her mom and started reading.

An hour later, it was time for the doctors' rounds, and Kia left, feeling bizarrely optimistic. She stepped off the elevator and into the lobby, where she ran into Hecate, just leaving the gift shop.

"Hey," Hecate greeted her.

"Hey," Kia responded. Hecate didn't look tired at all. Then again, Hecate didn't have to show up for school at eight-thirty that morning. Today she looked more like a woodland sprite than a creature of darkness, in light cotton coveralls and a pale blue shirt. Only the tattoo on her upper arm and the boots with multiple buckles said goth.

"So I guess you guys made it back into the city okay," Hecate said.

Kia nodded. "We had to work to stay awake till our stop, but we managed. We were totally wrecked today, though."

"Vampire hours," Hecate said. "If the vamps weren't already dead, the schedule would kill them."

Kia laughed. "That was an awesome place," she said. "I definitely want to go back."

"Cool. Glad you liked it. Your friends, though." Hecate shook her head. "They didn't seem so into it."

Kia's heart fluttered. "Well, you know. They just don't get it."

"Poor things," Hecate said with a grin. "But it's not everyone's scene."

Kia felt relieved. "Exactly."

"So . . . how's it going?" Hecate asked.

Kia knew that was Hecate's way of asking about her mom. "She seemed a little better today," Kia said.

"Excellent," Hecate replied. "That's all you can do, you know. Notice the good days."

"How about you?" Kia asked.

Hecate smiled, her wide eyes sparkling. "Gramps is going home! They think everything went A-OK. This could even be his last trip here."

"That's great," Kia said.

Hecate nodded. "Yeah. It's so different at home without him. Hey," she added, grinning. "We both have things to celebrate. Damon is spinning at Howling tonight. You know, the DJ from last night. Want to check out the vampires again?"

"Definitely," Kia said. She wasn't exactly sure how she'd get out of the apartment on a weeknight without her dad freaking or how she'd stay awake for another late-night thing, but she didn't want to pass up the opportunity.

"Why don't you come by the store?" Hecate suggested. "I get off around ten. Then we can head out from there."

"Sounds good."

Hecate gave Kia the address of NightTimes and then took off. Now all Kia had to do was figure out a way to bypass her dad.

No problem, as it turned out. At home, Kia found a message from her father saying that he had to head down to Washington, D.C., and wouldn't be getting back till the next day.

Perfect timing, Kia thought.

NightTimes was a small basement store down a rickety flight of stairs in the East Village. Kia could see Hecate through the window, sitting behind a cash register. She pushed through the door and little bells chimed. Hecate looked up from a catalog and smiled.

"Oh, good, this must mean it's almost closing time," Hecate said. "I am too bored."

"I'm a little early," Kia confessed. "I was hoping to find a better outfit." She had worn one of her long black dresses, but she really wanted something more hard-core.

Something more vampire.

"I can set you up, and I can give you my employee discount. Or," Hecate added with a grin, "if you promise not to spill or to sweat, we can just borrow you some looks."

Kia laughed. "I don't think I can promise either of those things, so we'd better stick to affordable stuff."

"No problem." Hecate came out from behind the counter. "Turn around," she ordered Kia.

Kia instantly felt self-conscious as Hecate's eyes roamed up and down.

"I know exactly what will be perfect on you." Hecate vanished into racks of black fabric. She emerged holding up a black dress with midnight blue trim. The body of the dress was corset-like, with lacings up the front and a full, short skirt.

Kia eyed the dress. It was going to be skintight. "Are you sure?" she asked. It was the kind of thing that she wished she was brave enough—sexy enough—to pull off.

"I am." Hecate handed her the dress. "And it will work great with the boots you're wearing." She pushed Kia to the dressing room.

"Oh, wait," Kia said, stopping suddenly. The dress was

sleeveless. Her track marks were still visible. "I'd love some long black gloves." She grabbed a pair from a basket on the counter. Then she continued into the curtained dressing room.

Kia stripped, slipped the velvet dress on over her head, and wriggled it into place, tightening the ribbons on the corset. She stepped back from the mirror and stared.

She looked amazing.

Her cleavage bulged above the corset line like a girl's on the cover of a romance novel. The skirt flared from her hips, hiding the thighs she regretted, and ended a few inches above her knees. Hecate was right. The dress was perfect for her, and her Victorian lace-up boots went perfectly with it.

The only flaw was the pattern of angry-looking red scratches up and down her arms. She pulled on the elbow-length gloves, and the look was complete.

Kia stepped out from behind the curtain. "Well?" she asked a little shyly.

"This is the look for you, babe," Hecate said. "You need to stick with the high Victorian stuff, not the grunge goth thing. You've got the body for it."

"Do I need more makeup?" Kia asked, admiring herself in the mirror. She was truly transformed. She looked older, more mysterious, and very, very sexy—rock goddess sexy. Sexy like she never knew she could look.

"Nah, you're fine."

Kia had put on heavy eyeliner and very dark lipstick. She had even powdered so that her face would be paler. She had designed a face on which fangs would not seem out of place.

Kia fumbled in her purse. "So, how much do I—"

Hecate held up a hand. "Let's see if it's returnable," she suggested. "If you get covered in a bloodbath, then we can talk."

"No," Kia said. "I don't want to return it. I want it to be mine."

Hecate shrugged. "Your call."

Kia pulled out the credit card her dad had given her. With Hecate's store discount she could buy the dress without even getting close to her dad's limit.

"And now—to the Lower East Side!" Hecate declared.

She shut off the lights, locked the door, pulled down the grate, and linked arms with Kia as they headed toward a bus stop.

"This scene is a little different," Hecate explained as they hopped off the bus on Delancey Street.

"How so?" Kia asked.

"The place is a lot smaller, a little more laid-back," Hecate explained, lighting up a cigarette. "Damon spins great music, and there's some dancing, but people also just hang out and talk."

Kia wondered what vampires talked about. Dental hygiene? Blood banks? How to avoid garlic? She shook her head—God, she was sounding like Aaron now.

They walked in without even getting checked by the door guy. They paid their five-dollar cover and headed toward the bar.

Once again, Kia was aware of the intense pounding of the bass track, the crash of the drums, the ability of the music to enter her body. She spotted a few faces from the night before— the red-eyed guy was standing at the bar talking to that

Queenie woman. And in the corner, surrounded by a console and speakers, was Damon the DJ.

He was startling to look at. So beautiful that Kia had to turn away. In the other nightclub, separated by space and an iron rail, she could observe him objectively. But close enough to talk to, to touch—he was too vivid. When Hecate handed her a drink, Kia led them to the other side of the dance floor. Away from the DJ booth, as far as they could get and still be in the room.

Hecate leaned against the wall and tapped her foot to the beat. Kia looked around the room, trying not to stare at the array of outfits, images, and personas on display. There were all-out Victorians, women with bustles and men with tailcoats and top hats. There were women in vinyl catsuits and men in leather pants and vests. There were guys and girls simply wearing black—normal, ordinary clothing, just black. There were fangs and tattoos and piercings and those bizarre contact lenses—and plain street makeup. Every variation seemed to be welcome; everyone talked to each other. People danced alone, in groups, or in tight clutches. The overwhelming impression Kia had was that once through those doors, the vampires would welcome you—whoever you were.

"They're checking us out," Hecate murmured. She held her drink toward two vampire boys standing near the bar. They were both in long black cloaks, with ruffled white shirts, tight pants, and high boots. Swashbuckling undead bookends.

In fact, Kia realized as she scanned the room, a lot of people were checking her out. She had never been the object of so much lustful attention before. It was a serious rush.

Kia finished her drink and smiled at the two swashbucklers. "Let's dance," she suggested to Hecate.

"You got it."

They moved onto the dance floor. Kia could feel eyes on her and it made her dance harder, more provocatively. Hands over her head, her spine supple, her head flung back, she tingled with what felt like promise, like hope, like absolute and total abandon.

She felt breath on her face and opened her eyes. One of the swashbucklers was dancing right in front of her, not touching her, but moving with her. Hecate was dancing with the other swashbuckler.

Kia wriggled up and down in front of her swashbuckler, and he imitated her movements. She let him put an arm around her waist and pull her into him.

Her eyes flicked to the console and the halo of fair hair above it. Damon's eyes roamed all over her—a body scan as palpable as if he were actually touching her. Kia licked her lips and thrust her hip at the swashbuckler, sliding her leg between his and arching back. He brought her back up to standing and kept his hands on her hips.

As the song changed, the swashbuckler moved a hand up to her throat, and only then she slipped out of his reach. She grabbed Hecate's hand and pulled her toward the bar, purposefully avoiding looking at Damon. Without the cover of the dance, her attraction to Damon felt too naked.

"I want another drink," Kia said, settling onto a bar stool with her back to the DJ console.

"I'll get those."

A handsome man with shoulder-length brown hair pulled some bills from his wallet. "Whatever these two want," he told the bartender.

"Yes, Lord Thanatos," the bartender said, his fangs hanging slightly over his lower lip.

"Two more bloodbaths," Hecate ordered.

"Right," Kia said. "And some water." The space was warm and close, and the dancing had heated her up.

"I am known as Lord Thanatos," the man said in a deep, rumbling voice. He had a strong square jaw and blue eyes outlined in black eyeliner. Kia judged him to be among the older group there, late thirties maybe. He wore a floor-length leather coat and a black turtleneck. His skin was pale, though Kia could see his pallor was achieved with thickly applied makeup, and his fangs were quite pronounced.

"I'm Hecate, and this is Kia."

The bartender placed the dark red drinks in front of Kia and Hecate. Lord Thanatos watched them, smiling, as they clinked glasses and took sips.

"Thanks," Hecate said.

"My pleasure," Lord Thanatos said. "It is always my goal to provide lovely young ladies like yourselves with anything they desire."

Hecate smirked. "Anything?"

Lord Thanatos smirked back. "Anything."

How about getting Damon the DJ to talk to me instead of you? Kia thought. She concentrated on her drink while Hecate and Thanatos chatted. She stole looks at Damon, hoping she wasn't being too obvious.

His head was bent over the console, his soft hair falling over his face. His tall, slim body swayed in time to the music, and he seemed completely in his own moment, oblivious to anything but spinning discs and enjoying the sounds. Then he glanced up and Kia found herself locked into his intense black eyes.

He smiled.

Kia forced herself to not look away.

She smiled back.

"Want another?" a voice said beside her.

Startled, she broke away from Damon's nearly hypnotizing gaze. "What?" she asked.

One of the swashbucklers from the dance floor was standing beside her.

"Your drink. Want another?"

"Sure." Then, feeling bold, she added, "And for my friend too."

"But of course," the swashbuckler replied. Once again, drinks appeared in front of Hecate and Kia.

Kia felt her third drink warming her veins, slowing things down, loosening her limbs. Swashbuckler was asking Kia about music and bands, but she had trouble hearing him over the loudspeakers, and besides, Damon had looked up again. It demolished her ability to concentrate on anything else.

He really was beautiful. Impossibly beautiful.

Kali, the woman with the purple-red hair, approached the console. Once again, she was dressed completely in white, and Kia noticed that the crowd parted to let her through. She and Damon spoke briefly, and then she circulated through the room again, people greeting her, trying to get her attention. She vanished into a back room.

Who is she? Kia wondered. She could tell by how the crowd was treating the woman that she was important, the center of . . . *something*.

The music changed again. Kia pushed herself away from the bar and strode onto the dance floor. Never taking her eyes off Damon, she danced.

She ran her gloved hand down the side of her face, along her neck, and across her chest. She bent her knees a little and rolled her hips. A guy came to dance with her, but she ignored him. He danced around her, and Kia felt as if she were some kind of goddess to be worshiped. It was incredible, like nothing she'd ever felt before.

Out of the corner of her eye she noticed that Damon continued to watch her, but he also watched the console. She didn't have his undivided attention.

Kia began to pay attention to her uninvited dance partner, hoping it would make it less blatant who she was *really* dancing for. The guy was kind of gawky, really tall and skinny—he reminded her of a vampire version of Aaron. Together they finished out the song.

"That rocked," the geek vampire said, his fangs creating a slight lisp.

"Yeah," Kia said. She was winded—the room was spinning slightly, making her wonder how many drinks she'd had, and she was sweating. She glanced at the console, but Damon was gone.

Disappointed, Kia lifted up her long hair to cool off the back of her neck and scanned the crowd for Hecate.

Suddenly something icy cold touched her neck and Kia let out a surprised yelp as chills ran down her spine.

A pale hand reached around from behind her and ran an ice cube along her forehead. Kia felt breath on her cheek and soft hair touching her skin. "This should cool you off," a deep voice said.

She twisted in the man's grip to see who he was and her legs went wobbly. Damon pressed against her back, holding her around the waist, pulling her into him. He lifted her long hair and brought the ice cube around to the nape of her neck again.

"I like how you dance," he murmured into her ear. "But I don't want you to faint from heatstroke. It gets very hot in here."

"Y-yes," Kia whispered.

He used a strong, cool hand to tilt her head, exposing the side of her neck. He ran the ice along her neck to her collarbone and back up again.

If his arm wasn't around her waist, she'd topple over. She tingled from the cold ice, his cool touch, and most of all his nearness. He was tall enough to lean against and even in her high-heel boots, her eyes only came up to his mouth.

His lips. They were so close to her.

"Open," he instructed, holding the ice cube above Kia's lips.

She did as she was told, and he slipped the nearly melted cube into her mouth. She rolled it around with her tongue, letting it cool her down even more. Only then did Damon release her.

"I'm Damon," he said.

"Yes, I know," Kia said.

He looked at her a moment, then grinned. "And you—?"

Kia flushed. "Oh. I'm Kia."

"Have I seen you before?" he asked.

"Last night. At Vampyre Central," Kia said. "You dropped red confetti on me."

He cocked his head as if he were trying to connect her to that girl from the previous night. "But you're new," he persisted. "To this scene."

Kia nodded.

"You seem to enjoy our dark world," he said.

Why was he talking to her? Could he actually be interested in *her*? Kia caught a glimpse of herself in the mirror behind the bar. She barely recognized herself and realized—yeah, maybe he could be interested in the girl she saw looking back at her.

She couldn't see Damon's reflection. He had to be standing in a blind spot. She wished she could see how they looked together.

She brought her attention back to what Damon was saying as it hit her that she hadn't heard a word. She was too distracted simply gazing up at him. Feeling him look at her. She couldn't remember ever being looked at with such intense focus before.

He must have been talking about some event because he pulled a card from his back pocket and handed it to her. Kia took it just as Kali came up behind Damon and tapped him on the shoulder.

He turned and she whispered in his ear, then he stepped away from Kia. "Break's over," he told her. She watched him follow Kali back to the console.

The world started up again. People moved around Kia, the

music blasted from the speakers, and she worked her way back to the bar.

Hecate grinned. "That was some meet-and-greet Damon gave you," she said.

"I know," Kia murmured. She could still feel his hands on her, her hair and neck damp from where he'd stroked her with ice.

"He must be into you," Hecate said. "I've never seen him pay so much attention to anyone new before."

"Really?" Kia's heart thudded. She looked down at the card he gave her. It was the same flyer Kali had given her the night before, to the "invitation only" party. "He gave me this."

Hecate nodded slowly and let out a little whistle. "Those are usually pretty hard to come by," she said. "Damon and Kali host some pretty serious stuff."

"Is she his girlfriend?" Kia asked, suddenly remembering how quickly Damon stepped away from her when Kali showed up.

"I think so, but I'm not sure. It's hard to tell sometimes. I've seen her give some pretty wicked bites to other people; him too."

Kia licked her lips. They felt dry; she felt fuzzy. The drinks had definitely been strong.

"Hey," Hecate said, leaning in close to Kia. She was talking a little more slowly and loudly than she had at the beginning of the night. "NightTimes is looking for another salesperson. You interested?"

"Really?" Kia turned to look at Hecate—the room tilted again and she clutched the bar. All better.

"Sure!" Hecate said. "It doesn't pay a lot, but you get a

decent discount and everyone drops off their flyers there, so you always know what's going on."

"Does Damon go there?" Kia asked.

"Yeah, he comes in sometimes." Hecate smiled. "Other cute guys too."

Kia looked around the room. They were all so beautiful. So intense. It was hard to imagine there was any world other than this dark place, this time set apart from everything and everyone else. This place where even death was not permanent, but a transition to another realm.

A woman moaned nearby and Kia turned to see a man in a long cloak biting her on the neck. The woman's head was thrown back, but Kia could see the rapturous expression on her face. On her other side, a girl about Kia's age was nibbling on a guy's wrist; each had their eyes closed in extraordinary concentration.

"Man, I think I need to go," Hecate said, wobbling a little. "You ready?"

Kia nodded. They wove through the crowd, past gleaming fangs and necks being offered and taken. A few people nodded at Kia and she realized they had probably noticed Damon paying attention to her. A gaunt man with long stringy hair grabbed Kia's wrist. "You are one of us now," he whispered hoarsely.

She slipped out of his grasp and followed Hecate outside. She felt assaulted by the outside world, by the rushing cars and the crowded buildings. They all seemed out of place—or maybe she was the one who didn't fit aboveground. The club was like a secret hideout, a place where she belonged.

"Do you—" Kia hesitated, not wanting to seem naive. "Do you think any of those people are real vampires?" As the words came out of her mouth, she knew how stupid they sounded. But she couldn't help it—everything that had happened in the last two nights had seemed completely real to her, no matter how many times she told herself it couldn't be.

But Hecate didn't laugh. She just shrugged. "Who can tell?" she said, weaving a little as she walked. "Maybe it's all about belief. Besides, if it looks like a vampire and acts like a vampire, isn't that enough?"

Maybe, Kia thought, stepping over a broken bottle. She thought about what Carol had said that time, about the laws of physics. *Belief.* Maybe that was all anyone needed.

SEVEN

Kia surfaced painfully from a groggy sleep to a room that was much too bright. Her temples pounded and her mouth felt as if she'd been chewing on socks. She squinted, saw the room spin, shut her eyes, and covered her face with her sheet.

She lay perfectly still, trying to hold back the whirlies, and thought about the night before. Maybe it was all the alcohol, but she couldn't remember feeling that light, that relaxed, that fully alive in a long time. And it wasn't just Damon—it was the whole thing. The dancing, the music, the costumes, the way she felt in her vampire attire. Bold, and proud, and as if anything she did was all right—with herself and with everyone there.

And Damon.

Kia rolled over and regretted it. She put her hand on her night table to steady herself and giggled. She knew it was just a hangover, but the idea that simply thinking about Damon set her spinning just seemed so . . . right.

She licked her dry lips and wished water wasn't so far away. *Hecate seemed to think he was into me,* she thought, taking in a long, slow breath.

It was hard for her to believe. A guy that hot—an older guy, a DJ, an older, vampire DJ with a following—was into *her.* Kia grinned. Even if they never went out, never kissed, never did anything more than have that one incredible encounter last night, knowing that she had grabbed his attention was enough.

Well . . . maybe one kiss would be good. Kia smiled again and sighed. *Or two. Or . . .*

A door opened and closed. She heard footsteps.

Kia blinked. Before she could decide what to do, her door opened.

"Kia, what are you doing home?" Her dad stood in the doorway, startled.

"I thought you were in Washington," Kia mumbled. He was talking too loudly and having to form words to answer him took a tremendous effort.

"I was. We finished early and I dropped by to get some files before heading over to the office." He stepped into the room. "Are you all right? You don't look so hot."

Kia shut her eyes. "Sick," she murmured. "I feel sick."

"Sick like you need a doctor?" her dad asked.

"Sick like I just want to sleep and not throw up."

"Sounds like the flu," her dad said. His brow furrowed. "Do you want me to . . ." He jiggled some coins in his pockets. "Should I stick around? Stay home?"

"No," Kia said. "I just want to sleep."

Her dad nodded. "Okay. Well, if you need anything, just call me at work."

Why didn't he stop talking? She wanted to be left alone to go back to thinking about Damon—and not throwing up.

"Can I get you anything?"

"Water," Kia croaked. "A big bottle of water."

"That's right. Fluids. That will be good for you. There's left-over wonton soup in the fridge. That might be good too. But you should order anything you want."

"Just water."

Kia shut her eyes and listened to her dad rummaging around in the kitchen. He came back into her room with a tall plastic bottle of chilled water. "Here you go, sweetheart. Take it easy." He sat on her bed. "Uh, I might be late again, but if you need anything, call."

Kia sat up carefully. The spinning was beginning to dissipate. She took the cold bottle of water from her dad and thought about ice.

He left, and she drank some water, then fell back asleep.

When she woke up a few hours later, she felt much better—even more after a long, hot shower. She came out of the bath-room and saw her dress from the previous night lying in a heap on the floor. As she hung it up, she stroked the velvet and decided she really needed to re-think her entire wardrobe.

The best way to do that would be to get that job at NightTimes. Employee discount and plenty of trying-on time—what more could a girl ask for?

The little bells jangled as she pushed through the door of the store. Even in daylight the place was dim. Hecate was marking price tags at the counter. She looked up, her almond eyes a little more raccoonish with dark circles under them.

"Hi," she greeted. "How's your hangover?"

"Alive and well," Kia said. "And yours?"

"I think I'm winning, but it's a close race."

"That was fun last night," Kia said.

Hecate nodded. "Yeah, that music rocked." She grinned at Kia. "But I think you were more impressed by the person spinning the sounds."

Kia covered her blush by rifling through some dresses on a nearby rack. Hecate stayed silent until Kia felt she had to turn around. "Okay," she admitted, encouraged by Hecate's warm smile. "So I like him."

"How could you not?" Hecate said. "He's hard-core yum. But Kia, watch out. There's more going on there."

"What do you mean?"

"He and Kali . . . I don't know what their deal is, but either way, the rumors are that they're into some heavy stuff."

"Like what?"

Hecate shrugged. "No one knows for sure. It's all inner-circle-type stuff. Only a select few are part of that scene, and none of them are talking."

"Hmm. So, were you serious about the job here?" Kia asked, wanting to get off the subject. She liked Damon, liked thinking about Damon, and wasn't really ready for anyone to give her a reason to stop.

"Definitely," Hecate said. "Stevo!" she called. "Someone here to meet you."

A short round man emerged from the back. He was

completely bald and looked like a little fat Buddha, except that he was tattooed and pierced on every inch of flesh that Kia could see. Probably in places she couldn't see too, but she had no interest in finding out.

"Kia is interested in taking Blanche's spot," Hecate said.

Stevo narrowed his eyes and walked around Kia.

"I'd really like to work here," Kia said.

"Have you done work like this before?" he asked, coming around her to face her again.

Kia decided she should stick with the truth. "No, but I'm a really fast learner, and I'm very responsible."

"Can you start tomorrow?" he asked.

"Yes," Kia said, figuring she would work it out.

"You're hired. Tell her what to do," he growled at Hecate before disappearing into the back.

The two girls high-fived. "You're in!" Hecate said.

"I've just doubled my wardrobe," Kia said. "Which is a good thing because I'm totally making myself over."

A series of little chimes went off in Kia's purse. She pulled out her cell phone and checked who was calling. Carol.

"Hi!" Kia said into the phone. "I was going to call you later."

"Where are you? I tried e-mailing, and I called the house," Carol said. "Are you okay?"

"I'm fine. I just had a little too much fun last night." Kia watched Hecate open boxes of amulets and tie little price tags to them.

"What do you mean?" Carol asked.

"I went out with Hecate again."

There was a slight pause. "To that vampire place?" Carol asked.

"To a different one." Kia picked up a pair of lace-up boots from a rack and checked the price. Ouch. Well, maybe with an employee discount . . .

"There are more of them?" Carol asked.

"Yeah. This club was a lot smaller, though." Kia held a maroon corset with black feather trim against her body and checked out her reflection in the mirror.

"Why would you go?" Carol asked.

Kia frowned. There was something unfamiliar in Carol's voice. A kind of incredulous disgust.

"Hey, good news," Kia said. "I just got a job!"

"Really?" Carol still sounded strange. Maybe it was just the cell-to-cell connection.

"Listen," Kia said. "Why don't I call you back when I get to a landline? I should get home anyway in case Dad calls."

"Okay. I'm heading home now."

"Later." Kia clicked off.

"So tomorrow," Hecate said, looking up from tagging. "I'll be here when you come in and I'll show you what you need to know."

"Cool." Kia grinned. "This is going to be great."

She hurried back to the Upper East Side, hoping that her father hadn't checked in while she was gone.

She'd still have to tell him about the new job, though. How could she explain that she went on a job interview when she was home sick from school?

The elevator door slid open on Kia's floor and the minute she was inside, she checked the answering machine. Safe. No calls from Dad.

She plopped down on the couch and dialed Carol.

"So like I said, I got a job!" Kia said as soon as Carol picked up. "With a paycheck and everything. Not to mention some serious perks."

"What kind of job?" Carol asked. She sounded like herself again. Interested. Kia could even hear a smile in her voice.

"At NightTimes, working with Hecate. Clothing store," Kia added, realizing Carol wouldn't know the place.

"Oh."

Kia frowned. Carol's voice had gone flat again.

"You should see the clothes, Carol," Kia pressed on. "They are so perfect for me, and I get a wicked employee discount."

"Well, that's good."

Way to sound enthused, Kia thought. She continued anyway. "And I'm making some cash, which means I can actually buy CDs instead of relying on Virgil to burn them for me. I can even get some techno-toys. And upgrade some paints and things . . ."

She stopped talking. Why was she trying to convince her best friend that getting a job was a good thing?

"What does your dad think?"

Kia sighed. "I haven't told him yet. But last summer he tried to make me get a real job instead of that art camp thing." Kia laughed. "If I had listened to him, I'd still be a virgin."

Now Carol laughed with her. "Yeah, there were definitely some perks for you with *that* job." She paused. "Do you ever think about that guy anymore? Kyle?"

"Not that much," Kia said, thinking back to camp, to the woods, to the itchy blanket and itchier mosquito bites. To the surprising, exhilarating experience of going a lot further than she'd intended but letting it happen anyway and then being more interested in trying things than Kyle had been. She figured once they'd done it, crossed that line, why hold back?

"He was okay," Kia said, remembering Kyle's definite ideas on what should and shouldn't come afterward, including having no contact once they'd left camp. "But it was kind of disappointing. Even though I *knew* I wouldn't hear from him again, I was still kind of hoping he'd call me after camp ended."

"You seemed pretty able to live without him."

"I guess . . ." Kia said. "So why are you asking me about Kyle?"

Carol didn't answer, and Kia sat up, holding the phone tighter. "Wait a sec, are you thinking of actually *doing* it?"

Kia never quite understood Carol's boundaries. She did all sorts of things with guys—more than Kia had done until last summer—but always stopped short of actually "going all the way." To Kia all the stuff Carol was doing counted as sex, but to Carol there was a vast distinction.

"I don't know. . . . Kind of. I think."

"Robbie?" Kia asked. Robbie was Carol's latest playmate—the cello player in band. Kia never thought Robbie had staying power; she'd seen Carol ditch guys and move on to the next one so fast she sometimes forgot to let guy number one know before she'd hooked up with guy number two.

Not surprisingly, Carol said, "No."

"Then who?"

"I haven't met him yet."

"So this is theoretical."

"So far."

"Then why? Just to check it out? I know you—you've held out for so long that finally doing it is going to have major impact."

"That's what I'm afraid of. I think maybe you had the right idea. Get it over with."

"That wasn't really how it was," Kia reminded her. "I liked Kyle. And it kind of . . . happened. We went overboard. I didn't plan it. Losing my virginity wasn't on my to-do list or anything."

"Yeah, I know you're right . . ." Carol said.

"You haven't met the guy yet," Kia said. "You need to wait for the guy who makes you tingle. Who makes you lose your concentration in class because you're thinking about his eyelashes or the way his fingers grip your waist." Damon's image flashed in her head and her blood stirred.

"Yeah?" Carol said. She sounded wistful.

"Yeah," Kia said firmly. "Otherwise it won't be worth it, and you'll feel sad. Because you've wasted that moment."

"Makes sense. Hey, you want to come over tomorrow?"

"I can't—I start at the store tomorrow after school."

"Oh, right." Carol was quiet a moment. "Is that going to work with school? And it's going to seriously cut into hanging-out time. Aaron is so psyched about this coven thing. He'll be disappointed if you vanish into the working world."

"It's just a job. It's not like I'm moving to another country or something."

"I guess," Carol said. "If Hecate works there, is it like a vampire store?"

Kia laughed. "Yeah, it's where people go to buy vampires."

"You know what I mean."

"Listen, call Aaron and we'll get together tonight. We can play his funny little Wiccan games."

"But your dad thinks you're sick."

"Oh yeah." Kia's brow furrowed. "I'll call him and find out when he's getting home. I'll call you right back."

"Hey, Dad," Kia said when her father's secretary connected her. "I'm feeling a lot better."

"That's good news, honey. So you'll be okay if I head back to D.C.?"

"For how long?"

"Just a day or two."

Wow, things were working out so easily. She could postpone telling him about the job and she could hang out as much as she wanted and meanwhile let him think she was doing *him* a favor letting him off the guilt hook.

"Definitely," Kia assured him. "You do what you need to do."

"Thanks, sweetie. Have I told you how proud I am of how grown-up you've become? This whole thing with your mom, and my traveling, well, I'm really impressed."

An uncomfortable tightness spread in Kia's chest. "Um, thanks. Have a good trip, Dad. Bye." She hung up the phone and stared at it.

Mom. With the new job, Kia wasn't going to be able to go to the hospital after school anymore. She might even have week-end shifts. Maybe Carol was kind of right: it'd be tough to squeeze everything in. But Kia could find a way, she was sure. Staying busy wasn't a bad thing, anyway.

And if Carol was worried that being friends with Hecate and

working with her at NightTimes was going to interfere with Kia's friendship with her and Aaron, Kia could work that out too. But if it was disapproval of the whole vampire thing . . . that was trickier. Because if Carol didn't approve of Hecate, she didn't approve of Kia either.

Kia decided to call Aaron to let him know she could come over. She set it up so that they'd meet after her dad came home, packed, and split for the shuttle plane.

"Hello, hello and help me," Aaron greeted Kia at the front door. His baby sister clung to his calf. He lifted his foot; she giggled and rose a few inches from the floor but didn't release him. "I've grown an appendage." He bent over, grabbed Miranda by the waist, and carried her over to the playpen. "My parents are out. Maybe we can use her in the ritual."

"Ritual sacrifice?" Carol asked, coming out of Aaron's bedroom. "Or as a ritual snack?"

Kia snorted. "And you tell me the vampires are too hardcore?"

Carol raised an eyebrow. "Uh, Kia? I was joking?"

"I hear you were out with the undead again last night," Aaron said, dropping some toys into Miranda's playpen.

So they'd been talking about her. "I felt undead this morning."

"Hence the absence."

Kia nodded. "I wasn't lying," she said with a smile. "I felt terrible. I'm fine now, though. Did Carol tell you about my cool new job?" She grabbed a stuffed elephant and tossed it into the playpen.

"At a store, right?" Aaron sighed. "Retail therapy that pays you. Sounds good to me."

"Carol doesn't agree with you," Kia said, noting Carol's frown.

"I just think . . . whatever."

Kia didn't push Carol to elaborate. Whatever she was going to say, Kia really didn't want to hear, anyway.

"What's the story with you and Virgil?" Carol asked instead. "He asked me today if you were all right."

Kia frowned. Maybe he wasn't as mad as he had seemed in school yesterday. "He's got some weird idea that he's supposed to, I don't know, *help* me or something," she said.

"I think he's into you," Aaron told Kia. "I've always thought that. And then when he started giving you those CDs, I knew for sure."

"Nah, it's not like that," Kia insisted. "The one time I thought maybe we were kind of on a date, I was wrong. Way wrong."

Carol put her hands on her hips and scanned the area. "Do we need all those candles and thingies again?"

"Definitely thingies," Aaron said. He went around the room setting things up.

With Aaron leading the way, they went through the same words and actions as they had the last time. Once they were sitting in the circle, they looked at each other. Kia giggled. "Sorry," she said. "I just don't know what we're supposed to do."

"Well, I do," Aaron announced. "I want to do a love spell. I am seriously crushed on that guy from the equinox ceremony."

"Elf Boy," Kia said.

Aaron cocked his head. "I think I'll call him by his real name. Otherwise I might wind up with little gnomes and brownies stalking me."

Carol nodded. "From what I've read, you've got to be really specific for spells to work correctly."

Aaron's eyes widened. "Okay, now I'm nervous. What if I mess up a spell and it has the opposite effect? Or it makes the wrong person fall for me? Or I fall for the wrong person?"

"That sounds like most romance," Kia said. "All those Mr. Wrongs."

"Let's just give it a try," Carol said.

Kia watched curiously as Aaron got his materials together— a pink candle and an orange candle. A seashell, some lavender, and a rose.

"I call upon earth, air, fire, and water to draw to me the one I want," Aaron declared. "I light a pink candle for romance and an orange candle for communication." He lit the candles, then rubbed the lavender between his fingers, releasing a soft scent. He dropped it into the seashell, then plucked the petals from the rose and added them to the lavender. "I offer lavender and rose petals to the goddess Venus to help me to win Elf Boy—"

Kia snorted.

Aaron glared at Kia. She covered her mouth.

"I mean *Michael Feinburg's* attention and affections. As I say it, so it is."

He blew out the candles. Kia watched the trails of smoke rise into the air and vanish, supposedly the method of transport for Aaron's wish.

Aaron rocked back on his heels. "That felt good." He turned to Carol. "Next?"

Carol lit the orange candle. "I call upon earth, air, fire, and water to open the lines of communication between my brother and my parents."

Kia glanced at Carol. Her voice was shaky and her eyes were shiny.

"And if that's too much to ask . . ." Carol took in a sharp breath. "Then please have Roger get in touch with me. I just want to . . ." She paused a minute and swallowed. "I want to talk to him." Her shoulders slumped.

Aaron reached out and took Carol's hand. She didn't look at him; she just stared at the orange candle. "As I will it, so it will be." She blew out the candle.

They sat quietly for a moment. Kia sensed the sadness in Carol and wasn't sure what to do. Roger was either going to get in touch or he wasn't; he was either okay or wasn't. But at least from what they knew, he was doing fine. He just was doing it far away and on his own terms. Roger had made a choice. The great big world versus his continually pressuring family. Kia knew which she would choose.

Carol blinked a few times, then looked at Kia. "What do you want to do?"

Kia pursed her lips as she contemplated the candles. "Nothing."

"You don't want to do a spell?" Aaron asked.

"I just . . ." Kia shrugged. "I just don't feel it is all. Now that we're doing it, it seems . . . silly."

Carol bristled. "Silly?"

"Nothing personal. I mean, it's cool with me if you guys are into this magic stuff."

"It's not any sillier than people dressing up and pretending to be vampires," Carol said.

"That's different," Kia protested, not wanting to get into it.

"How?" Carol asked.

Kia ran her hands through her hair, tugging at a snarl. Why was Carol pushing this? "Because . . . I don't . . . Because it is."

Carol rolled her eyes.

Miranda started to whine, and Aaron decided it was time to close the circle. The air seemed charged, and things felt prickly between her and Carol, so Kia figured the best thing to do was get out of there.

As she walked home, Kia couldn't get Carol's words out of her head. As much as she hated to admit it, Carol had a point. Why would someone dress up like an undead creature—and not just for Halloween?

Vampires weren't real . . . were they?

She hopped on the crosstown bus and found a seat. Wouldn't it be cool if there really were such creatures, though? To *be* such a creature?

To fear nothing, to live forever, to not worry about mundane things like school, and grades, or even death. Just pleasure, and going after what you wanted no holds barred; just experiencing the blood in your veins and the blood of another. *Blood is life, so of course the undead crave it.*

She glanced down at her arms, visualizing the fading tracks underneath her long sleeves, less than a week old. She shut her eyes and didn't open them again until she was facing out the window. The tip of the Metropolitan Museum of Art appeared through the trees as the bus emerged on the East Side.

In medieval times, maybe even later, people believed they could be cured by bloodletting. Was that what she was doing when she cut herself?

Vampires went after other people's blood; they didn't spill their own. Kia smirked. Maybe that's what she ought to be doing—instead of releasing her own blood, her own essence and life energy, she should be drinking in the blood of others.

The thought traveled through Kia like a cold chill, snapping her out of her slouch.

Maybe a vampire wasn't some kind of supernatural creature but a human with the desire for blood. By the time she reached her stop, Kia wasn't sure if she was scared or exhilarated by the idea.

EIGHT

It worked!" Aaron grabbed Kia in a bear hug and squeezed. The difference in their heights meant that her nose was crushed into his skinny chest. She wriggled out of his grip and stumbled backward.

"What worked?" she asked. She gazed up into his beaming face. She couldn't remember seeing him smile so hugely since before the acne invasion last summer.

He beamed back at her. "The spell."

Kia glanced around self-consciously, seeing if anyone had heard Aaron.

"What do you mean?" she whispered. They headed into school.

"He e-mailed me last night. After you left. After the spell. We're going to hang out this weekend!"

"That's great!" Kia said, stunned.

"It's proof that magic works," Aaron said. "Since we both

know it couldn't have been my good looks alone that grabbed him."

Kia looked down at her shoes, embarrassed by how close to her own thoughts Aaron's self-deprecating comment was. Then she looked up and smiled. "Maybe so," she said, "but it will be your charm that hooks him."

Aaron laughed. "Later," he said. "I'm going to float off to class now and fantasize till Saturday."

"Have fun," Kia said. She watched him lope through the hallway, dodging students.

Huh, she thought. *Aaron dating. Weird.*

She was genuinely happy for him, but Aaron had never dated anyone. He'd always been Kia and Carol's main companion. She wondered what it would be like if Aaron and Elf Boy got serious.

At lunch Kia moved her tray through the line and then found her friends at a table near the windows.

Carol glanced up and then looked back down at her smoothie. She seemed to be concentrating on stirring it very carefully with her straw. "So I guess Aaron told you about his weekend plans?"

Kia slid into the chair opposite Aaron. "He sure did."

Carol looked up at her, her blue eyes challenging. "So now do you believe that magic is possible?"

"Do you?" Kia hadn't realized that Carol was taking this all so seriously.

"I do," Aaron said, with a firm nod. "Why else would he e-mail me?"

"Maybe he likes you all on his own," Kia suggested.

"I'm keeping an open mind," Carol declared. "Maybe it's for real, maybe it isn't. We have to keep working at it. We start with the hypothesis and then test it. Verify it through repeated experiments."

Kia unwrapped a granola bar. "I didn't think your mind was so open at the vampire club."

"That's not the same thing."

"Yeah? Why not?"

"Those are freaks dressing up and working out some deep dark secret inner weirdness."

Kia's jaw hardened. "So I guess I've got some deep dark inner weirdness going on. That's why I like the clothes Hecate picked out for me. Why I like the dancing. And the guys I met there."

"That's not what I'm saying," Carol protested.

"Hey, all of our weirdness is right on the surface," Aaron jumped in. "Nothing inner. Nothing deep and dark. Just right out front wacko."

Kia's eyes involuntarily flicked to her long sleeves.

"And hold on, you met guys there?" Aaron asked. "With fangs?"

"Some." Kia didn't want to get into it. Not when Carol had made her disapproval so clear.

"So when does your job start?" Aaron asked.

"Today," Kia replied. "So if you need any warlock drag, I bet I can find you something there."

"She's working from four to ten during the week," Carol said, tapping the end of her straw. "Will you be working weekends too?"

Kia felt as if she were being interrogated for a crime. "I don't know yet. The schedule is going to get worked out today. But yeah, probably." She crunched her granola bar. The dry crumbs made her cough and she quickly opened her bottled water and took a swig.

"She hasn't asked her dad," Carol added.

"Do you think he'll be pissed?" Aaron asked.

Kia wiped her mouth with her napkin. "Why would he be?" she snapped. "Carol's the only one who seems to have a problem with it. Most parents *want* their kids to get jobs."

"Maybe . . ." Carol mumbled.

Kia stared at her, then down at the lipstick-smeared napkin. She smoothed it with her fingers, trying to restore its original perfectly square shape.

"How about your mom?" Aaron asked. "What does she think?"

Now Kia felt a pang. This job *was* going to interfere with visits—that part was true and the only part that made Carol's objections have any sting.

"I haven't told her yet. I want to see if I last the first shift," Kia said, folding the napkin in half.

"You'll be great," Aaron assured her.

"Yeah?" Kia smirked at him. "Seeing as I've had no job experience, what would make you think that?"

"Because when you do something, you do it full-on," Aaron said. "You've always been that way. Once you're in, you're in all the way." He shrugged. "If you like this job, you'll be taking over the store in no time!"

"Thanks," Kia said, flashing a quick smile. She stood up. "Well, I should do some work in the studio since I start my shift later. Don't want to fall behind in my drawing portfolio," she added with a slight edge for Carol's benefit.

"Right," Carol said. "That's good thinking."

God, Kia thought, *when did she turn into a parent?*

Kia tossed her garbage and slammed her lunch tray onto the rack. She left the cafeteria, knowing she'd be the topic of conversation between Aaron and Carol for the rest of lunch.

At five minutes to four, Kia walked into NightTimes. Stevo glanced up from the cash register. "Yes?" he asked.

"I'm here for my shift," Kia said, raising her eyebrows.

"Oh, right. Hecate, your friend is here to work," he bellowed. He looked at Kia. "She'll tell you what to do. I like employees to not bug me for every little thing. Figure it out yourself. Your job is to make mine easier."

Hecate came out from the back. "Hey, Kia."

"Hey," Kia replied.

"I'm going," the manager said. "Hecate leaves at eight. I'll be back at ten to lock up."

Now Kia felt really nervous. She hadn't realized she'd be in the store by herself on her first day.

"Don't worry," Hecate whispered. "By the time I go, you'll know everything there is to know. He just likes to think working here is complicated." In a louder voice she added, "I'm going to start by showing her the stockroom, okay?"

Stevo nodded.

"Don't mind him," Hecate said as they went into a back area filled with boxes. "He's really not so bad."

Hecate gave Kia a rundown of where things were, then

brought her back out front to show her how to use the register. Kia spotted lots of flyers for club nights on a counter and notices posted on a bulletin board by the front door. She remembered the "invitation only" flyer that both Damon and Kali had given her. The party was being held tonight.

She felt a pang of regret. She was way too chicken to go to the event on her own.

"Things get busy around now," Hecate said, interrupting Kia's thoughts. "That's why there are always two of us here from four till eight. Then it quiets down. At least weekdays. Weekends it's just busy whenever."

Kia nodded, hoping she would keep things straight. Luckily the calculator did all the math, a lot of the stock was already tagged, and the book prices were on the books.

"Some kids do steal," Hecate warned. "So keep your eyes open. Just make sure they know you're watching."

Kia had no idea what she would do if someone tried to take something. Maybe the job was a mistake—too much responsibility.

"We get first dibs on the cool stuff," Hecate said. "Like this." She held up a black vinyl catsuit with red lightning bolts down the sides. "I'm putting this away for me!"

The door chimes jangled.

"Your first customers!" Hecate grinned. "Luckily, since we're a goth place, Stevo doesn't mind if we give attitude. So ignore them if you want—just keep your eyes open."

Kia laughed. "That's good. I don't think I could be one of those super-friendly Gap types."

"Me either. That's why I like you. We're both brilliantly hostile."

Two girls and a boy who looked to be around Kia's age wandered through the racks. Hecate started tagging some boots and Kia stood at the ready at the cash register. Eyes open, just like Hecate had said.

The boy was cute, in a rumpled way—black skintight pants, a pierced eyebrow, and a studded dog collar, worn with a crumpled white ruffled shirt. Kind of a mixed metaphor—poetic goth or something. Both girls with him wore long dresses with clunky boots. The boy looked up from the rack of jackets and caught Kia looking at him.

She immediately looked down at the cash register and pretended to be busy. One problem with keeping an eye on the customers—they thought you were checking them out.

She glanced at him from under her eyelashes, not moving her head. He had gone back to browsing, but now he was smiling.

He came up to the counter with a jacket. "I'll take this," he said.

Kia nodded. She had to remember Hecate's instructions about how to use the register.

"Do you go to Sinful?" he asked.

"Never heard of it," Kia said.

"You should check it out," he replied, handing over a wad of bills. "I play there on Mondays."

"Yeah?" Kia said.

"My band." He jerked his head toward the two girls, who were now cooing over ankhs and pentagrams in the jewelry case. "They're in it too."

"Oh." Kia folded the jacket and shoved it into a plastic bag along with the receipt. She handed the bag to the boy.

"I can get you in free," he added.

"Cool."

The guy left, trailed by the girls.

"Your first sale," Hecate said.

"And I didn't even screw up." Kia fluffed her bangs. "*And* my first attempted pickup in the workplace."

"Ooh, baby, believe me, it has only just begun," Hecate said. "This is one wicked sitch to meet delectables in. And get free passes."

"I think I'm going to like it here," Kia said.

The next few hours were pretty slow—high school students wandering in and not buying anything. Then, as it grew later, the after-work crowd started showing up.

As the sun set, the store slowed down again, so Kia decided to try on the midnight blue dress with the laces up the front and the back that had caught her eye the moment she entered the store. She came out of the dressing room to show Hecate and stopped.

Damon and Kali stood at the front door.

Damon leaned against the wall as Kali walked to the shoe section in the back. He was adjusting the zippers on the cuffs on his jacket. Backlit by the streetlamp outside and contrasting with the dark night sky, his fair hair and pale skin seemed almost otherwordly—an angel in black leather, complete with halo. He turned and broke the illusion, the streetlight casting dramatic shadows on his chiseled face. Kia took in a sudden breath: he was that beautiful.

He must have heard her because he looked up and smiled. "Hello. Again. And so soon."

"H-hi." Kia cleared her throat. She didn't trust her voice, so she didn't say anything else but made herself smile, pleased that she'd chosen this moment to put on the blue dress.

His black eyes were on her, all over her; she could feel them. She wondered if he looked at everyone that way. Or did he see something special in her—something he wanted to keep looking at?

"That looks great on you," Hecate said from the cash register.

"Yeah?" Kia asked.

"Yeah," Damon answered instead, a sly grin on his face. "Very great."

Don't blush don't blush don't blush. "Then I guess I'll have to buy it," Kia said.

"Wear it next time you're at Vampyre Central," Damon suggested. "And I'll spin some discs just for you."

"Will you cool me off again?" Kia said, amazed at her ability to talk to this demon-angel. *It must be the outfit,* she decided.

"If that's what you want," Damon said, a teasing tone in his voice. "Unless you prefer heating up."

Kia played with the end of one of the laces, not sure how to respond.

"Do you want to keep it on till the end of the shift?" Hecate asked.

Damon cocked his head at Kia. "You work here? Why haven't I seen you before?"

"It's your vampire hours," Hecate joked. "You only come in after the sun goes down."

Damon laughed. "That must be it. There's a lot you miss when you can't risk daylight."

"Actually," Kia said, "this is my first day. Night," she added, glancing at the dark street outside.

Kali came up front to join them. "I like those thigh-high silver numbers," she said. "But not at that price. Are they going on sale anytime soon?"

Hecate shook her head. "Too new."

In the bright light of the store Kia could see how heavy Kali's makeup was. She was still quite beautiful, with her fine features and amazing body, but her undead complexion was definitely applied with a sponge and a powder brush. The thick eyelashes—obviously fakes—were missing, as well as the fangs. Damon, on the other hand, was naturally pale. Even here, away from the club, his skin seemed nearly translucent.

"Oh, hello," Kali said, as if noticing Kia for the first time.

"Hi," Kia said quietly.

Kali nodded at Kia. "I tried that on," she said.

"Oh?" Kia wasn't sure how to interpret that comment.

"It suits her more than it did you," Damon said. "Don't you think?"

Kali just kept nodding. "Yes. She looks positively scrumptious."

"Exactly my thought," Damon said, looking at Kia, his dark eyes much more intense now, no tease or smile in them.

Goose bumps prickled her skin as if a cold wind rippled past her. It would be impossible for her to look away. Even if she wanted to.

The door opened and a group of kids piled in, setting the chimes jangling.

"See you again," Damon said. He swept Kali out of the store.

Someone poked her in the back. Kia jumped.

Hecate grinned up at her. "Hello? Come back to earth, little missy."

Kia flushed and gazed down to the floor. "That obvious, huh?"

"Oh, big time," Hecate said. "Still, it didn't seem all on your side."

Kia's heart thumped a little. "So, I'm not crazy? He seems interested?"

"He looks at you as if you were candy. Or a pint of blood, I should say."

"As long as I look tasty," Kia said, grinning. "Good enough to bite."

"Yeah, and then Kali will come after you with her own sharpened incisors," Hecate replied.

Kia winced, feeling herself deflate. "So is she his girlfriend?" she asked.

"I told you, I'm not really sure what the deal is with them. Other than that they're both pretty deep in the vampire scene."

"What does that mean?" Kia asked.

"Do you have these in a size ten?" Kia's head jerked up at the familiar voice. Virgil appeared from the back of the store, holding a pair of boots. He must have come in while she was changing into the dress. He stopped when he saw Kia and fiddled with the boots.

This is awkward, Kia thought. She'd gotten away with ignoring Virgil at school for the past two days. And now here he was, clearly waiting for Kia to set the tone.

Kia caught a glimpse of herself in one of the many long

mirrors dotting the store. She remembered Damon's attention, his eyes on her. She felt strong, powerful, desired. She
figured she could afford to be generous.

"Hey, Virgil," she said.

"Kia." He sounded wary.

"Listen, sorry I went ballistic on Friday," she said, choosing to
take the high road.

He relaxed his shoulders. "Well, I probably did something
wrong, only I didn't know it."

"Kind of," Kia said. "But you couldn't know, really."

"What are you doing here?" he asked.

"Working," Kia replied.

"Since when?" Virgil looked surprised.

"Today," she said.

Three girls from Kia's school came in through the door.
They were the popular girls of the goth clique that Virgil was
always sitting with at lunch. She wondered if they had planned
to meet up with him in the store.

One of them—the petite Asian girl with a furious haircut
and angrier makeup—did a double take when she saw Kia.

"Hi, Julie," Virgil greeted the girl. He nodded at the other
two with her. "Mandy. Wren."

Julie studied Kia. "So you work here?" she said.

"Yup."

"Interesting," Julie said, nodding.

"I wish I had such a cool job," said the tall girl, Wren. "I work
at the copy shop near school." She rolled her eyes. "So boring."

"Yeah," Mandy added. "You're lucky, Kia."

Kia shrugged. "I guess."

"Have you figured out your term project yet?" Julie asked.

The three girls talked with Kia about school and about bands, and she pointed out the new flyers on the counter. Virgil stood nearby, hands in his pockets, jingling his change.

"Hey, we should split," Julie said. "The music store is going to close soon."

"See you at school tomorrow," Wren said. "I can give you the history notes for the class you missed."

"Thanks," Kia said.

Virgil lingered after Julie, Wren, and Mandy left. "I burned a new CD I think you'll like," he said.

Okay, now *he's acting normal.* "Cool," she said.

"Yeah, so . . ." He rocked on the balls of his feet. "So, later."

"Yeah, later."

Virgil gave her a quick, furtive smile, then left the store.

"Ooh, he likes you," Hecate said.

"What? Virgil?" Kia shook her head. "We're just friends."

"If you say so." Hecate began packing up her stuff to go.

Kia felt a flutter of anxiety. "You're leaving?"

Hecate smiled. "Don't worry, you'll do fine on your own."

Hecate left and Kia sat behind the cash register, thinking over her first shift.

Even if there was something romantic between Damon and Kali, it couldn't be serious, Kia decided. Maybe they hooked up sometimes, but it couldn't be a steady, exclusive thing. Not with Damon pointing out to Kali how hot Kia looked. No boyfriend would do that to a girlfriend. Especially since Kali agreed with him.

She fiddled with the keys on the cash register, thinking

about how Julie and her friends had been so friendly. This job was dead center in the serious goth scene—not just the little school clique. And Kia was in the heart of it. Julie and the others must have a whole new impression of her.

And Virgil. Maybe Hecate and Aaron were right and he did like her. After all, Kia had thought that maybe the pizza thing was a sort-of date. But what did that really change, at this point? Virgil was nice enough, but next to Damon, a high school boy was, well, a high school boy. And Damon was so much more. . . .

She shivered, a strange thought flitting through her brain, one that teased the edges of her mind. Damon was more, maybe, than she'd even realized.

NINE

Kia did a quick once-over of NightTimes before she started shutting everything down for the night. The whole lock-up routine had become a natural habit so easily, it was hard to remember how nervous she'd been during her first shift three weeks ago.

"Ready?" Hecate asked, waiting at the door.

Kia was about to say yes when her cell rang. She glanced at it and saw Carol's number appear in the display. Kia paused, biting her lip. She didn't really have time to talk, and she didn't want to have to explain to Carol where she was headed. Things had only gotten weirder the past couple of weeks with Carol. She just couldn't seem to deal with Kia's job or with all her club nights with Hecate. Kia hadn't even been eating lunch with Carol and Aaron the past week because she was sick of the awkwardness whenever it came up. She'd been sitting with Virgil and his goth friends instead.

"Are you getting that?" Hecate asked.

"Nope," Kia said, clicking off her phone. "If it's important, she'll call back." She stashed the phone in her purse, then did a quick mirror check before meeting Hecate at the door.

Hecate flicked the lights and locked up. They headed to the Lower East side.

"No vamps tonight, right?" Kia asked as they let several taxis barrel past them down First Avenue.

"Well, none out," Hecate confirmed. "This club is basic goth."

"You're sure Damon will be there?" Kia asked as they crossed the street. If she was going to risk snoozing through her morning classes, she wanted to be sure she had a good reason.

Hecate laughed. "You have that boy on your brain."

"More like in my blood," Kia admitted.

Hecate gave Kia a quick glance, and Kia looked away. She didn't mean for that to come out quite so intensely. Every time she'd seen Damon—at the store or the vampire events Kia and Hecate frequented after work—there was an undeniable charge between them. She noticed he found ways to touch her—passing her on the dance floor, saying hello at the bar. He'd brush up against her or slide a hand along her waist and down to her hip. But it never progressed beyond that.

Kia was dying to talk to him more, to explore the connection and see where it could go, but so far she hadn't had the chance. Tonight, maybe? She honestly didn't feel as if she could go much longer without having him close to her—the need was so strong, almost familiar in a strange way.

They stopped for a red light and Hecate lit a cigarette.

"Damon spins at regular goth nights too," she said. "I guess there aren't enough vampires around to keep him in bloodbaths and rent, so he branches out."

Inside the club, Kia did her automatic scan for Damon. She finally saw him leaning against the wall near the bar, scoping out the scene. His stillness was riveting. Several guys Kia recognized from NightTimes waved to her and Hecate.

"Go ahead," Kia told Hecate. "I'll catch up with you."

As Hecate headed for the table, Kia homed in on Damon. He hadn't seen her yet.

"Kia!"

Julie rushed over to Kia. Wren and Mandy followed her. "Love the dress," Julie said.

"Thanks," Kia replied. She peered over Julie's shoulder. Damon was gone.

"Will you hold some earrings for me?" Wren asked. "I saw them yesterday at your store, but I didn't have any cash on me."

"Come by when I'm on and I'll put them aside for you," Kia said, nodding.

Kia tried not to be obvious, but while Julie, Wren, and Mandy chatted about clothes and school, she kept her eyes out for the only person whose presence she really craved.

"Hello," a deep voice said behind her.

A slow smile crawled across Kia's face.

Damon.

Kia turned and smiled at him. "Hi," she said. She was aware of Julie, Mandy, and Wren all standing there waiting for her to introduce them, but she didn't say a word.

"Hello, ladies," he said, looking past Kia.

"Hi," Julie said.

"Yeah, hi," added Mandy. Wren just stared with her mouth open.

Kia wanted him all to herself. "See you around," she told the girls.

They took the hint and wandered away.

"You look good," Damon said. Kia felt her whole body flush. "I'll play some songs for you. Things you'll recognize from Vampyre Central."

"That's cool," Kia said. "This place is a little . . . tame."

Damon raised a pale eyebrow and cocked his head. "You think so?"

He gripped her waist, pushed aside her hair, and hovered, his lips inches from her neck. Kia froze, waiting for what might happen. He stayed absolutely still until her neck practically screamed for him to bite her. Then he took in a deep breath and stepped away. "No," he murmured. "I shouldn't."

He released her and headed for the DJ booth, never looking back. Kia stared after him, trying to quiet her pounding heart. Eventually she gave up and surrendered to the beat.

"Kia, I'm very concerned."

Kia sat in the fake leather chair in the school guidance counselor's office a few days later. One leg crossed over the other, her booted foot jiggled with impatience. Halloween was coming and the cutout jack-o'-lanterns and black cats decorating Ms. Rodriguez's office made her feel as if she were trapped in middle school. Not even. Elementary.

"Throughout October, I've noticed a rise in absences," Ms.

Rodriguez continued. "And I spoke with several of your teachers. They are also concerned. Your performance has slipped during this same period." She folded her hands on top of a file folder and looked at Kia. "Has something happened?" she asked.

Kia picked at her nail polish.

"Kia?" Ms. Rodriguez prodded.

"Not really," Kia said.

How could she explain how much everything had changed? That she'd found a new group of friends who understood her, who appreciated her. A place where she could go and be with creatures like herself who craved the dark, who embraced their power, who sought pleasure with each other.

How could she explain that everything had changed because of how Damon looked at her?

"I understand that there have been some changes in your living situation," the counselor said. "Your father is now your custodial parent?"

Kia sat up straighter, her attention yanked from her Damon reverie back to the cramped office. Was Ms. Rodriguez saying that she was going to call her dad?

Luckily the case in D.C. had kept Kia's father out of town most of the time over the last month, and she always made sure to call him to check in. What did he know? Care? As long as she wasn't causing him trouble, he was fine.

A phone call from school would be considered trouble.

"You know why, don't you?" Kia asked, making her voice soft and pathetic. She leaned forward in her chair, clasping her hands, rattling her bracelets. The tracks had faded, so she was able to wear short sleeves and bracelets again. It had been over a month since she cut—or even had the urge.

"Why you've started living with your father?" Ms. Rodriguez asked.

"It's my mom." Kia made her voice quaver, as if she were about to cry. "She—she's dying."

The counselor's brow furrowed. "I'm sorry. No, I wasn't aware of the circumstances." Her voice had softened too.

Kia licked her lips; they had suddenly gone dry. So she was using her mother's cancer to get out of trouble. Hell, it was true—even if her mother wasn't actually *dying.*

Besides, if I can get some good out of this ridiculously awful situation, why shouldn't I?

Kia took a deep breath. "Sometimes I—I go to the hospital. Just to . . . you know . . . see her."

Kia's stomach went funny. Maybe that was too much, going too far. She had barely been to the hospital lately. She made phone calls, sure. But between NightTimes and her nightlife, Kia had very little time to spare. She was amazed she made it to school at all.

Mom's okay with it, she told herself. She tugged at the collar of her shirt. For some reason, her chest felt tight. Her mom had always been saying Kia spent too much time at the hospital, and she got tired so easily on Kia's visits anyway. Kia slowed down her breathing so that she could hear what Rodriguez was saying.

"Kia, I understand your need to see your mother. But she'd be the first to tell you that school is important too. Please try to limit your visits to after school and weekends."

Kia nodded. "I know I should," she said, sounding very young.

"Good. I'll make a note in your file that this is a . . . *challenging* time for you right now, but it won't help your mother if your schoolwork suffers."

"You're right," Kia said, nearly making herself sick with how pathetic she could sound.

"And Kia," Ms. Rodriguez added, "I realize this is an incredibly difficult time, but we do have to think about your future here. If things continue this way, I'll have to contact your parents so we can discuss some possible ways to help you out. The end of the semester isn't so far away, and the further behind you get, the harder it will be to catch up."

"I'll do my best," Kia said. "I promise."

"Thank you. And—I'm sorry about your mother. If you ever need to talk about it . . . remember, I'm here."

Kia left the office, forcing herself not to smirk. That was so much easier than she thought it would be. The tight feeling rose up in her stomach again. Maybe she could stop by the hospital before work.

"Kia!" Aaron practically mowed her down as he came around the corner.

They grabbed arms and she regained her balance. "What's the rush?"

"Rehearsal." He nodded toward a room down the hall. "I'm late. You in with Rodriguez?"

"Yeah. But I worked her and everything's okay."

"*Is* everything okay?" Aaron asked. "I feel like you've vanished."

Kia shrugged. "The whole job thing . . ."

"And you're hanging more with Virgil and his gang," Aaron

pointed out. He grinned mischievously. "So was I right? I always thought the two of you would hook up. If I was into dark, brooding, and straight, I'd go for him myself."

Kia laughed. "Just friends. Speaking of hookups . . ." For a moment she wanted to ask if Carol had taken the plunge with anyone yet but decided it would be too weird to hear that from Aaron. Besides, Carol would have told her.

Well, maybe. Kia suddenly realized that their phone conversation about virginity busting had been their last serious talk. That was over a month ago. Since then it was mostly small talk around school, a few e-mails. Carol hadn't left a message when she'd called Kia's cell the other night, and Kia had never called her back.

Aaron cocked his head. "Yes . . . ? Exactly what are you asking, Miss Nosy?"

Kia scrambled and came up with a new question. "Elf Boy. What's going on there? Are you going to elope and live in the fairy kingdom together?"

Aaron fake-smacked her arm. "Hey—I'm the only fairy who can call me a fairy."

"I was making a magic allusion," Kia said, laughing. "But anyway, are things going okay there?"

"Actually, yes." Aaron bounced on the balls of his feet as if he were having trouble staying earth bound. "We've been hanging out a lot."

"Excellent. So is he a boyfriend?"

"As in going steady, dinner and a movie—"

Kia cut him off. "No. As in hot and sweaty and then all sweet and romantic."

Aaron sighed. "Not quite. But I have hope."

It was amazing to think that this whole thing between Aaron and Elf Boy began with a Wiccan ceremony. Maybe there really was something to magic after all. From Kia's recent experiences among the vampires, she was willing, hoping in fact, to believe anything was possible.

"Maybe you need to do another spell," Kia suggested.

"I've done them. How do you think I got this far? It's not like this is a face that would launch a thousand ships. Well, maybe it would, but they'd all be fleeing in the opposite direction."

"Stop it." Kia hated hearing Aaron cut himself down.

Aaron leaned against the wall and hooked his thumb under the strap of his backpack. He ran his fingers up and down the strap. "We have done some messing around, but just a little," Aaron confessed.

"That's a start."

"Yeah. He's fun. So are his friends."

It occurred to her that if Aaron was spending time with Elf Boy and his pals and she was hanging in Vampville, then Carol might be feeling a little left out. "Is Carol cool with you and Elf Boy?"

"Sure, why shouldn't she be?"

Kia shrugged. "No reason."

"I guess we haven't been spending as much time together," he said, his strawberry blond eyebrows coming together. "But she seems okay with it. She's really busy preparing for the end-of-semester concert."

"Oh, right." Carol always disappeared into rehearsals around this time every year. Kia felt the tension in her chest ease. She probably barely noticed Kia and Aaron hadn't been around as much.

"Hey, we should get together," Aaron suggested. "You, me, and Carol. Do another ritual."

"I don't know. . . ."

"I think it's important. To . . . reconnect. Renew our bond." He ran a hand through his red hair. He needed a haircut, and for the first time Kia noticed pale reddish stubble on his cheeks. "We really haven't hung out in a while."

I should do this, Kia decided, feeling guilty. Besides, that time they had done a ritual for Kia's mom, it had seemed to have some effect.

"Well, if it works for Carol, tonight works for me," Kia said. "I need to go to the hospital now, but we can meet after that. Call my cell and just tell me when."

Kia rode the bus from the hospital crosstown to Aaron's that night, feeling a knot of anxiety in her stomach. It had not been a good visit. It wasn't so much that anything bad had happened, just more of the same—more weakness, more exhaustion, more doctors, more hair loss, more vomiting, more apologies, more regret.

Her mom had been so happy to see her that Kia felt awful that she'd come so infrequently in the last month. And then when Kia had inadvertently revealed that her dad was spending most of his time in D.C. on his big case, her mother had become as indignant as her wasted state allowed. Upsetting her mom was the last thing Kia had wanted to do.

Kia stepped off the bus and hurried to Aaron's building. A cold gust of wind hit her; winter was definitely on its way. She shivered on her way into the lobby and realized she was shivering on the inside too—just a little.

Why was she so nervous? It was just Aaron and Carol.

But she knew better. Things had changed between the three of them.

She rode up the elevator, got out, and buzzed Aaron's doorbell. *It doesn't have to be this way,* she thought. Vampires respected other worlds; Mundanes should be able to do that too.

Aaron greeted her in his kimono and ushered her into his room, where Carol was sitting on Aaron's bed. She looked up from a book of spells when they entered the room. "Hey," she said.

"Hey," Kia replied.

Kia perched on the edge of the bed while Aaron bustled around, setting up. "So what's on the program tonight?" Kia asked, trying to warm up to the evening's plans.

Carol shrugged. "I can't decide."

"How did that last performance go?" Kia asked, embarrassed that she had never asked. It had been weeks ago.

"Brilliantly!" Aaron responded for Carol. "Right?"

"Really?" Kia asked. "Weren't you having trouble with one part of it?"

Carol nodded. "It was so strange," she said. "We did a spell, and afterward I breezed through that measure as if it had never been a problem."

"I told you," Aaron said, kneeling on the floor and lighting a candle.

"Wow," Kia said.

Carol laughed. "Of course, I have brand-new problems to solve."

"Don't we all?" Aaron said.

A tiny smile tweaked the corners of Kia's mouth. For the first time, she felt as if she had fewer problems than before.

Then a queasy feeling crept through her. Her grades were basement level, her mother wasn't any better—in fact, she seemed worse—and Carol and Aaron felt like unfamiliar territory.

She shook off the unpleasant clutch in her stomach by remembering Damon's black eyes, his cool, pale hands. By remembering she had a place to be, a place to go, a person to become as often as she needed to. Best of all, she could go bare-armed if she wanted without any fear at all. Her biggest secret had evaporated.

Carol was discussing spells, trying to decide whether to try to find herself a new romantic playmate since Robby the cellist was over or if she should strengthen her breath control for the upcoming concert.

"Boy toy," Aaron said. "Obviously. Let's get our priorities straight."

Kia forced herself to join the conversation. "Carol doesn't need spells to get boys to crawl all over her." She smiled at Carol. "Go for the music."

Carol smiled back. "Yeah, you're right. Better use of energy."

Kia noticed they didn't ask her if she was going to do a spell. Maybe she would, maybe she wouldn't. After all, the spells seemed to have worked for Aaron and Carol.

She decided to suspend her judgment and give herself over to the game.

She felt a pang. *In other words, don't be Carol.*

Her eyes flicked to Carol. She was bent over a book, her long auburn hair cascading softly across her face. Once again, she looked pretty, nearly posed, as the candles flickered around her.

She can't help it, Kia realized. Carol was afraid of the darkness. That was why she was *pretty*—not beautiful. But Kia knew that Carol's limits weren't her fault; everyone was taught to fear their shadow selves. The vampires had shown Kia that.

Carol must have felt Kia's eyes on her because she looked up, puzzled, and gave her a tentative smile. Kia reached out and took her hand, feeling compassion for her friend's fears. Carol's smile broadened. She squeezed Kia's hand.

Aaron stood hovering, watching, holding back his glee. Kia released Carol's hand. She was about to really make his day.

"Do you have another one of those kimono jobs?" she asked.

Aaron blinked at her. She nearly burst out laughing at how surprised he looked. Then he recovered. "Sure do. One with your name on it."

After Kia slipped into the kimono, they cast the circle and started doing their spells—Aaron trying to get more action going with Elf Boy, Carol to strengthen her flute playing and her singing.

"So do we do our chanting now?" Aaron asked.

"Wait," Kia said. Her body thrummed with vibration from the ritual. "I, uh, I want to try."

Aaron and Carol glanced at each other.

"What do you want to do?" Aaron asked.

She suddenly felt shy, now that her friends were looking at her expectantly. "For my mom," Kia said. She took a deep breath. "Something to help my mom."

Carol took her hand; Kia could feel the warmth radiating from her. "Sure."

Kia looked at Aaron. "So is there a spell in one of those books that I should try?"

"There's some stuff you can use, but I think the magic works best if it comes from you. Make up your own words," Aaron said.

"I—I don't know if I can do that," Kia said.

"We'll help you," Carol offered.

"Quick, before you change your mind!" Aaron placed a blue candle in front of Kia. "This is for healing."

Kia nodded and knelt in front of the candle. She lit it and stared into the tiny flickering flame. She sat for a few minutes and then started to feel stupid. "What should I do?" she asked.

Carol picked up one of the spell books that lay on the floor near the bed. She flipped through it, her brow furrowed. "Maybe some kind of banishing spell? To get rid of your mom's illness."

Kia nodded.

"It will be even stronger if it becomes like a chant," Aaron suggested.

"Okay," she said hesitantly. She hadn't realized it would be this complicated.

"This is for purification." Aaron pointed to a white candle. "Like I said, the blue one is for healing. And here's a red one for strength and courage."

"That sounds right," Kia said.

"Why don't you light the candles and then talk about what you want to get rid of? You should have an action too," Aaron added. "To act out banishing the things you want to banish."

"I know!" Kia grabbed a blank yellow pad from Aaron's desk. "Okay if I destroy this?"

"Go for it."

"Let's re-center," Carol suggested. "Get back in the flow thing."

Aaron had them hold hands and shut their eyes. They sat in silence, breathing quietly, more and more deeply. Kia let herself sense Carol and Aaron beside her, the energy flowing between them. She let herself connect to . . . *something* . . . the way she had that night at the Wiccan ceremony, the way she always felt at the clubs.

Maybe this will work.

"Ready," she declared.

Carol and Aaron opened their eyes. Kia knelt in front of the three candles and lit a match.

"For purification." Kia lit the white candle. "For healing." She lit the blue candle. She took a deep breath, then lit the red candle. "For strength and courage."

"What do you want to banish?" Aaron asked.

Kia stared at the blue candle. "The bad cells in my mother's body," she said. Her voice shook a little.

"Repetition is important," Aaron said softly. "What do you want to banish?"

Kia cleared her throat. "The bad cells in my mother's body," she said more loudly.

"What do you want to banish?" Aaron repeated, and this time Carol joined in. It was beginning to sound like a chant.

"The bad cells in my mother's body," she said.

"What do you want to banish?"

Kia found herself standing, clutching the notepad.

"The bad cells in my mother's body." She ripped a piece of

paper from the pad, crumpled it, and stomped on it. "The bad cells in my mother's body," she shouted. She knelt back down and ripped the paper to shreds. "The bad cells in my mother's body."

Aaron and Carol kept chanting and now they started clapping and stomping their feet. Energy was building. "What do you want to banish?"

Kia ripped another page. "My mother's pain! It hurts to see her that way. I want to take it away. Take it away."

She fell to the floor and pounded on it. "She's so afraid. I'm afraid too. I don't want her to be scared. I don't want to be scared."

"What do you want to banish?"

"Please make it stop. Make it all stop. I want to go back to when it was all okay. I'm not okay. It's not okay."

"What do you want to banish?"

Kia tore at the pad, ripping it, tearing at it, smashing her hands against the floor, pounding in rhythm with Carol and Aaron's chanting. Feelings tumbled around inside her, propelled by the increasing intensity of Carol and Aaron's voices. They shouted louder and faster and faster, and Kia's voice became a wail over the din. Something burst open inside her. "I can't do this," she shrieked. "I don't know how to do this. I can't handle it. I don't want to. I don't want to anymore!"

Aaron's voice faltered, and Carol continued alone. "What do you want to banish?"

"Everything. I want to banish everything." Kia rolled into a ball and sobs poured out of her. She clutched the ruined notepad to her chest and hid her face. Carol and Aaron had stopped chanting and clapping. Her eyes were shut and she had no idea what they were doing, thinking. She felt humiliated and raw, crying uncontrollably on Aaron's floor. As her sobs quieted, anger replaced agony: she felt furious that Carol and Aaron had pushed her to this.

After what felt like an eternity, Aaron said, "We send Kia's banishing spell out to the universe. As we will it, so it will be."

Kia rolled back upright and wiped her face. She avoided looking at them; she just stood up and straightened the kimono. "I—I've got to go."

"We need to open the circle," Aaron protested, but he hadn't even completed the sentence when Kia disappeared into the bathroom to change back into her clothes.

Screw them and their witch games, she thought. That was too intense, too weird.

She dressed quickly and burst out of the bathroom.

Aaron cleared his throat. "Um . . ."

"Are you okay?" Carol asked.

"Yeah, sure." Kia slung her bag over her shoulder. "Gotta go."

"Kia," Aaron said. "I—I didn't think it would be . . . I didn't know."

"Yeah, right." Kia crossed the room, and Aaron and Carol both made way for her. She could feel them wanting to stop her.

"Kia," Carol said. "I'll go with you."

"No," Kia said. She opened the door and whirled around to face them. "I'm okay. Really."

She spun back around and left.

Her veins pounded, throbbed, called to her. *Cut me, release me, let it out, let it all out.*

She needed a blade, needed the sharp searing sudden pain, the slow ooze. *Let it out let it out let it out.*

Her pace was quick. She was already at the bus stop. She flung herself up the little steps, swiped her card, and lurched into a seat. An itch, a cry. She pressed against her wrists, trying to stop it, trying to quiet it all down. Columbus Avenue. Central Park West. The bus kept stopping and Kia urged it forward. She had to get back to the apartment, now, take care of this need now. Grab the delicate edge and go at it. Now. Through the park and out the other side. Fifth Avenue. She could feel her eyes burning with unshed tears. Madison. Park.

I don't want to feel this. I don't want to do this. As powerful as the need to cut was, so was the need to not succumb, not give in. But how? How could she stop herself? She had never been able to before. Not when the craving was so powerful.

She saw the green globes indicating a subway stop. She was at Lexington.

"Getting out," she shouted before the bus could drive away. She hurtled out the door and down into the subway.

Her breathing became calmer once she was on the train. *It will be okay,* she thought as she watched for her stop. *You'll be okay. Everything will be all right.*

TEN

Wind whipped along the wide and deserted streets of Brooklyn, ruffling Kia's hair, stinging her eyes and making them tear. Her feet pounded the broken pavement as she hurried away from the trendy streets toward the desolate area near the river where the clubs were. Her ears tingled with cold and from the strain of trying to hear the music, her body aching with the need to cut, the need to dance.

That's the fastest I've ever made it here from the subway, she thought, arriving at the entrance to Vampyre Central. She opened the door, briefly wondering where Scream the doorman was.

She stood at the entrance, blinking. Something was horribly wrong.

The music blasting wasn't the goth, synth, dark wave undulating and hypnotic beats and music filled with rage, outrage, despair, and dark beauty. This music was bouncy, guitar heavy, chord chimey, voice twangy, and hard on Kia's ears.

And the people! Kia saw cowboy boots everywhere she turned. Cowboy hats. Ruffled skirts, a sea of denim, bandannas, and big hair.

She stumbled backward, reeling from the bizarre sight. She put out her hand to steady herself on the door frame.

A woman in a gingham top tied at the waist, skintight blue jeans, and pink cowboy boots approached her.

"Can I help you?" the woman asked, obviously confused by Kia's presence.

"I—I think I came on the wrong night," Kia said.

"We're only here once a month," the woman said. "Classic country."

Kia nodded. "Oh."

"So, I guess you won't be staying," the woman added. It was definitely a statement, not a question or an invitation.

Not that Kia wanted to stay. Not even a tiny piece of her littlest toenail wanted to stay in that club. "Nope!"

"Hope you find what you're looking for," the woman said as Kia turned to go.

Now what? Frustration, disappointment, and fear tumbled around inside her. She gnawed on her nails. They had to be somewhere, right? He couldn't have just vanished.

Her shoulders sagged. Damon was the one she was really after. It was Damon she had wanted to turn to, be comforted by. That was crazy and she knew it. He wasn't her boyfriend; he was barely her friend.

But maybe he could be. Maybe, if she opened up to him, he'd open up to her. Maybe, if she could just get into his arms, into his orbit, his inner circle, she could get into his life.

Kia ran her hands along her arms, trying to warm up, trying to quiet the noise in her veins. She squeezed first one forearm, then the other, as if the pressure would soothe her need. It didn't.

She had to find him.

She walked toward another club she'd been to with Hecate, but when she approached the entrance, she saw that the door was locked and the lights were off. She stared at the metal grate covering the door. *Where else could he be?* She had no idea where he lived, no idea what he might do on a night he wasn't spinning discs.

The clubs in Manhattan. On the Lower East Side. He sometimes worked there too. She walked quickly back to the subway.

Kia waited on the platform a long time. It was late and the L train wasn't exactly reliable. She paced, trying to remember the addresses of all the venues that hosted vampire events. By the time she emerged back in Manhattan an hour later, she had managed to figure out a map in her head.

Hope returned when she saw some vampire types hanging around in front of a small bar. It was amazing how much better she felt just seeing them.

She made her way inside. Vampires were sitting at small tables, talking. Some stood at the bar, a few nuzzled in the booths by the velvet-curtained windows. The room was fairly dark, with candles, and none of the fancy lighting and fog effects in the dance clubs.

Music was playing, and Kia scanned for Damon, but she didn't see anything resembling a DJ booth. She went up to the bar and when the bartender came over, she asked, "Who's your DJ?"

"You're looking at him." He jerked his head toward a small CD player on the back bar. "Double duty. You'd think they'd pay me more."

Kia nodded, realizing that the guy was just playing whole sides of CDs, not actually mixing. No Damon here.

Unless he's just hanging out . . . ?

She stayed for a while, knocking back a bloodbath to calm her nerves, then nursing another to stall, hoping Damon would come in.

Finally, giving up, she went in search of the next place on her mental list.

The alcohol had warmed her, so she walked at a more leisurely pace, checking out shop windows, peering at the variety of people on the street. The Lower East Side was much busier than where she'd been in Brooklyn.

She turned a corner and gasped. There he was.

His back was to her, but she recognized the halo of fair hair illuminated by the streetlight he leaned against. He wore his usual long black leather coat, tight black jeans, and pointy black boots.

Kia's heart leapt at the sight of him. Then it clutched as she wondered if he was there waiting for someone.

As if he sensed her, he slowly turned around, a smile already on his face in greeting.

"Kia."

Hearing him speak her name, seeing his smile, looking into those dark eyes made her freeze mid-step. She realized that he remembered her name and felt bold.

"Damon," she said strongly.

He didn't move. "Come here," he said softly. "Closer."

Up close, he took her breath away. She could feel power emanating from him. She felt the buzz of her intense attraction to him and then realized that it was a current they shared. He wanted her too.

"Am I close enough?" she asked.

Damon looked down at her, his face serious. "For now," he said.

Kia looked away; she couldn't take it, his gaze was just too much, her desire too obvious. She didn't want to make a fool of herself. Damon put his hand on her face and forced her to look up at him again. Her skin tingled at the touch of his cold hand. She shut her eyes and let herself feel his fingers, his closeness.

"Something's bothering you," he said.

How does he know? She didn't trust herself to speak, so she just nodded.

He let his hand drop to her throat. "You are much too lovely to be upset." He slid his hand down her body and found her fingers. "Come on, what you need is distraction."

Mutely, Kia let Damon lead her down the street. She didn't care where they went.

His cold, strong hand sent a crackle of excitement through Kia, energizing her. She felt ready for anything. At the corner, he ducked into a doorway, yanking her into the enclosed space with him. He turned his back to the street and leaned over her.

Is he going to kiss me? Kia wondered. She kept her head down, unable to look into his intense dark eyes. *Breathe,* she reminded herself.

"Are you cold?" he murmured in her ear. He opened his

long leather coat and pulled her into it, bringing the sides around her back. She was completely enveloped by his presence, yet he wasn't holding her, he was holding his coat. His mouth was inches away from her face, but he wasn't kissing her. He was pressed up so close to her body that she could feel his belt buckle through her jacket, his rough sweater scratching her cheek. Touching but not touching.

She couldn't answer. She could only shut her eyes and wish that they could hold this moment, this embrace that felt protective, and sexy, and dangerous all at once.

She heard people walking by, their clicking heels, their chatter. It was hard to imagine a world beyond Damon's shielding body. After they passed, Damon glanced over his shoulder and stepped away from her. "Let's go. You probably need to warm up. Standing still won't do it."

He looked up and down the street, picked a direction, and pulled Kia along with him.

A thought suddenly flashed into Kia's Damon-drenched brain: Was he avoiding those people who passed by while they were in the doorway? Was that why he pulled her in there—so they wouldn't see them?

What did that mean? Did he not want to be seen with her? Or did he just not want to be seen—period?

They passed several stores, lots of bars, multiple restaurants without speaking. Kia couldn't tell if Damon had a destination in mind or if he just wanted to keep moving.

She didn't care.

She was with him, he was holding her hand, he was leading the way. That was all that mattered.

She wasn't alone with her throbbing veins.

The moment she had the thought, she realized the urge had passed. The only pull she felt now was toward Damon.

"Damon! Hi!" A gaunt man with long, stringy hair, wearing a top hat and a heavy overcoat, emerged from a shadowy stoop.

Damon stopped. Kia was thrilled that he didn't let go of her hand.

"It's me," the man said, shambling closer. Kia could see that he was one of the vampires who not only had fangs but also those funky contact lenses. His were yellow, with black slits in the center. "Don't you remember?" the guy continued. "Rex Notorious. House of Xantho."

"Sure," Damon said. "Rex."

Kia had the feeling that Damon either didn't remember Rex or didn't want to.

"Hey, man, where's the scene?" Rex asked. He swayed a little. "The Mundanes are out in force tonight. Need to find our kind."

"Sorry, can't help you," Damon said. "Night off."

"Got a smoke?" Rex asked.

Damon shook his head.

Rex nodded, his eyes narrowing as if he were remembering something. "Oh yeah. You don't smoke. Drink either, from what I hear." He laughed. "Gotta stay pure in some way, right?"

Kia glanced at Damon. Now that Rex mentioned it, she had never seen Damon drink or smoke. Damon didn't respond.

"I've seen you before," Rex said, leaning toward Kia. He smiled a slow, creepy smile. He tilted his head toward Damon. "He dances with you. I've seen it. You must be a tasty morsel if you're one of Damon's chosen."

Damon stepped slightly in front of Kia; nothing obvious, but enough to make Kia feel protected and for Rex to take a step back.

"No problem, man," Rex said. "Not moving in. If she's your designated, that's cool. Haven't heard of you siring before, though. Thought that was Kali's area."

Kia could feel Damon bristle beside her. He seemed to be working very hard to keep himself under control. She didn't understand what Rex was saying, but it was clearly pissing Damon off.

"But hey, whatever. It's all cool with me," Rex said, oblivious. "Not my business if you're blood-bonded or not."

"That's right," Damon said coldly. "It isn't."

Rex held up his hands, making his extreme manicure apparent. His fingernails were long and curved and painted black. "No offense meant, man. I mean it."

Damon stared at Rex, his black eyes never leaving the gaunt man's face. Rex grew more flustered and grabbed his forehead. "I'm sorry, man. I didn't mean anything, I swear."

Damon didn't say a word. He just kept his focus on Rex.

"I'm out of here," Rex said, stumbling backward. "Just don't—I didn't—"

Rex broke off, turned, and hurried away down the street. Only once he disappeared around a corner did Damon turn his attention to Kia.

"Sorry about that," Damon said, his voice low, his eyes dark and somehow sad.

Kia shook her head. "It's not your fault that he's so weird."

Damon took a finger and gently moved a strand of hair out

of Kia's face. "No, but it still shouldn't have happened. You were already having a hard night. I wanted to distract you from that. And instead . . ."

Kia shook her head and took his hand. "Don't. Don't be sorry. For anything."

Damon smiled, and Kia felt her knees go liquid. His beauty was astonishing. The sharp lines of his gorgeous, extravagant bones, the almost feminine mouth, the blackness of his eyes, which were such a contrast to the pale, wispy hair. It was a face almost too beautiful to be human.

"Damon?" A girl's voice broke the current between Kia and Damon. He glanced over his shoulder, then he turned all the way around.

"Meredith," Damon greeted the woman, who looked to be in her late twenties.

"You're not working?" Meredith asked. Her heavily made-up eyes gave Kia a quick once-over, then she ignored her.

"Not tonight."

Meredith licked her lips. "I know of a party—"

Damon cut her off. "No thanks."

Now she frowned. She flung her long purple hair over a shoulder. Kia wondered if it was a wig. "Fine," Meredith snapped. She stalked away.

Damon shook his head. "Let's get out of here," he said. "There are just too many people I know around here and I could seriously use a break from all of them." He turned to face Kia. "Ever feel that you need to escape your own life?"

"Always," she said softly. Her eyes flicked down to the ground.

Damon took a step closer and cupped her cheek in his cold palm. She pressed her face against his hand, and he put his other hand in her hair. "Yes, I think you do," he said, his voice husky. He stroked her hair as if she were a cat he was petting.

He made no move to lift her eyes to meet his. Kia stared at the pavement and let herself feel the softness of his fingers.

"Where do you live?" he asked.

"Uptown," she said.

Did he want to come home with her? Her heart sped up and she broke away. "I don't want to go home. Not yet."

Damon nodded. "Well, let's get you back to that neighborhood at least. I could use a change of scenery."

He stepped out into the street, raised an arm, and a cab appeared. He opened the door, gestured for Kia to get in, then slid in beside her.

"Where to?" he asked.

She really didn't want to show him where she lived—what would he think of the snooty doormen and the perfectly manicured shrubs in front of her high-rise? And how was she going to tell him she couldn't bring him home without saying that she was still only in high school?

She realized he and the cabdriver were waiting for her to give directions. "Fifth Avenue," she said. "At Seventy-second Street."

The cabbie did a U-turn and screeched up First Avenue.

Damon looked at her, as if trying to put together the address with her appearance. "You really *are* an uptown girl."

"I like it over near the park," Kia said. She couldn't tell if he approved or not. Mostly he just seemed puzzled.

It seemed strange to be doing something so ordinary—riding

in a cab—with someone as exotic and mysterious as Damon. As if they were two regular people on a date.

Are we?

"I can sense something dark in you," Damon said, sliding closer. He draped his arm across the top of the seat. Kia leaned back so that her neck rested lightly on his arm. He stroked her shoulder. She shut her eyes again, willing him to kiss her.

She could feel his breath on her face. "Are you?" he whispered. "Dark?"

What is he asking me? she wondered. There was a darkness inside her, a darkness that frightened her—but didn't frighten him. In fact, he seemed to like it. She arched her back and reached up for him, wrapping her fingers around his neck. She pulled his face toward her, those lips that were mere inches away, down onto her own. He held back a moment, his neck slightly stiff under her hand, then she could feel him give over to her.

It was the most power she had ever felt in her life.

As his tongue spread her lips apart and his grip on her shoulder tightened, her mind and body split. Her hands, her mouth, her muscles, her skin all took on a life of their own while her mind spiraled with thoughts: *I did this. Damon's tongue is in my mouth, his hands are clutching me, and I made it happen.*

He pulled away first, leaning back against the seat, but his arm was still across her shoulders. She watched him as he looked away from her and gazed out the cab window. His silence and turned face frightened her, and she thought about biting the back of his neck—it tempted her all on its own, and besides, maybe it would make him kiss her again. But she restrained herself.

The cab pulled to a stop and Damon slipped his arm away from Kia as he reached into his coat pocket. She fumbled in her purse and pulled out some bills.

"I've got it," he said, handing money to the cabdriver.

She sat huddled by the door, wondering if he was going to get out with her or not. Maybe she shouldn't have kissed him?

He glanced at her. "This is the right place?" he asked.

"What?"

"So, are we getting out?"

"Right. Sorry. Just . . . distracted." Kia smiled tentatively.

He smiled back and she felt a flutter between her ribs.

The street was empty at the entrance to the park, and Kia wondered how late it was. It had to be well after midnight. The full moon hung low in the dark sky, but the city lights and streetlamps made it impossible to find any stars. She still reeled from kissing Damon, from feeling a kind of hunger for her in him. It made her giddy and she was afraid she'd giggle, or stumble, or blurt out something ridiculous. No one had ever had an effect like this on her before. No one.

Kia stared up at the inky expanse and took in a deep breath of frosty air. Her lungs filled with the cold night air and she suddenly felt wide awake.

She felt him watching her, waiting for her to do something, take him somewhere. There were stone benches along the park wall, and she took his hand, intending to lead him to one. All she could think of was getting her hands back on him.

"I haven't been up here in years," Damon said. "I wonder how much of the landscape I remember."

Kia had always been warned to never go into the park after

dark, but with Damon she felt no fear, just exhilaration. As they walked deeper into the park, she realized that they were near the Great Lawn, where she, Carol, and Aaron had participated in that first Wicca ritual. She flashed back to earlier in the evening when she'd freaked out at Aaron's because of that stupid spell.

Tugging Damon's hand sharply, she pulled him to a stop and slid her arms inside his open coat. She pressed against him, her fingers clutching the back of his sweater, and she kissed his neck.

She felt him moan more than she heard him, and it made her brave. She continued to press her mouth against his skin, to lick him, to nibble her way around his throat and up to his mouth—and then they were kissing again.

He pulled away this time too, but he kept his arms around her. "You are very, very tempting," he said.

"I'm glad," Kia said.

"That's not always a good thing," he said, smiling. "It makes things dangerous."

"You don't seem afraid."

"Oh, but I am," he said, stepping away. He held up his hands as if he were trying to protect himself from her. "I'm terrified, can't you tell?"

Kia laughed and they started walking again. The park was quiet, and the deeper inside they got, the farther away the world seemed. It was just Kia and Damon. No one else. Just how Kia wanted it.

"I've noticed you usually come in with Hecate or alone," Damon said. "Most of the others travel in packs."

Kia looked down at the ground so he wouldn't see her huge smile. He'd noticed her! He'd been paying attention!

"Shows confidence," Damon said.

"I guess," she said.

"Sometimes they seem so . . . tiresome," Damon said.

"Yeah," Kia said, not quite sure what she was agreeing with.

"Like tonight. I just got sick of it." He looked down at her. "And then I ran into you."

"And . . ." Kia bit her lip. "And you don't think I'm . . . tiresome?" She held her breath.

"I wouldn't be with you if I did. And I wouldn't have traveled so far uptown." He laughed and took her hand.

Kia felt her chest expand.

She wanted to ask him about the strange things that Rex and Meredith had said earlier. They were probably the kinds of people he was talking about. The *tiresome* ones.

"That guy Rex," Kia said, trying to figure out how to ask Damon about siring and blood bonding without sounding stupid. She'd heard the words in the clubs before but had never paid that much attention. Now she wished she had.

"Exactly," Damon replied. He shook his head. "Rex Notorious. What a joke." He grinned down at Kia. "He gives real vampires a bad name, don't you think?"

Kia stumbled on the path, and Damon gripped her arm to steady her. "Careful."

He was joking, Kia told herself. He was making a joke.

"I mean, really," Damon continued, guiding Kia more carefully over the uneven pavement. "What most of the people in the scene don't seem to get is that a real vampire wouldn't pro-claim it so openly. Not at such public events."

"Well, sure," Kia said. "Right."

"Not any self-respecting vampire, that is."

"What?" Kia asked. Was Damon telling her that he was . . . real?

Damon took a sharp right, leading Kia under one of the many stone bridges that dotted the park pathways. It was pitch-black under the bridge and smelled bad too. Damon didn't seem to notice; in fact, his pace slowed, while Kia's heart sped up. It was creepy in the darkness.

She heard a skittering movement and saw a pair of small gleaming eyes ahead of her. Her body tensed and she gripped Damon's cold hand harder.

He squeezed back. "It's just a rat," he said quietly.

Oh, that's all, Kia thought. She didn't trust herself to speak— she was afraid she'd squeal with fear.

"Hello, fella," Damon said as he passed the rat. It stood absolutely still, as if frozen. Even the sound of Damon's voice didn't startle it. It seemed almost tame. Or mesmerized.

They came out on the other side of the dark bridge and con-tinued along the path to the lake. Damon sat on one of the benches and pulled Kia onto his lap. He took her face and gently turned it toward the lake. "See the moon? It's gone swimming."

He was right: the full moon's reflection on the lake seemed to be underwater. "It's beautiful," she murmured.

"When I first got to New York, I used to come here a lot," Damon said. "I liked this spot."

And he brought me here to share it. Kia's body nearly went limp with desire for him. She felt as if she were melting.

He played with her hair, gazing at the jagged rocks across the lake, up at Belvedere Castle. "It always reminded me . . ." His voice trailed off, as if he decided he shouldn't say anything more.

It was brighter in this spot; without the cover of trees the full moon could shine down on them, and the streetlamps were closer together. Kia could see a number of turtles at the edge of the lake scurry into the water and swim for the other shore.

She leaned against Damon, wondering what it was that he saw, what it was about the castle looming above him that drew him here. She realized she had no idea where he came from, where he grew up.

She moved her head to see his face—he continued staring straight ahead. Sometimes he looked just a few years older than Hecate, maybe twenty-five at most. But right now, he seemed much, much older. As if he'd seen too much, experienced more than he should have.

The way I feel.

His dark eyes flicked to her face, his brows furrowed, and he shifted her on his lap so he could really look at her. "You're sad again."

She nodded but didn't speak, amazed by how easily he could read her.

He touched her cheek, his fingers even colder than her face. "You don't have to tell me," he said. "We can just sit here."

She leaned into him, hiding her face against his shoulder.

He tightened his hold on her. "Whatever it is that's making you sad. It's why you don't want to go home."

Kia nodded into his neck.

"I get that." He let out a long slow breath. "Believe me, I get it."

Kia turned and her mouth brushed his jaw. This time Damon turned the gesture into a kiss; his fingers tangled in her hair, and as the kiss grew deeper and more intense, he slid her off his lap. Once she was beside him on the bench, he somehow shifted her back up onto him so that she straddled him. His hands pressed hard on her hips, pulling her down onto him. Their breath became ragged, became moans, and Kia knew that she would do anything he asked her.

They pulled apart a moment; Kia wanted to see his beautiful face, to remind herself that he was real, that she was really with Damon. Her eyes flicked to a movement behind the bench. She gasped.

A row of rats sat behind them. Watching them.

"What's wrong?" Damon asked, trying to pull her back down to kiss him.

"I—I—" She shuddered.

Damon released her and moved her off him. "You're right. This is not a good idea."

"No!" she yelped. "It's—" She turned to look at the rats again so she could explain. They weren't there anymore. Had she imagined them?

"Come on, it's late." Damon stood up and held out a hand.

"What?" Kia stared at him.

"I'll get you back to your place. Can't risk sunrise, you know," he added, grinning.

Kia smiled back weakly. "Of course not."

They walked back in silence, the only sound their hard heels hitting the pavement. Kia kept her eyes on the ground, not wanting him to see the struggle she knew was playing across her face. Her cold fingers fiddled frantically with the lining of her coat pockets as she desperately tried to think of something to say.

Was he mad at her? The idea made her stomach churn. Those stupid rats. Her feet scuffed pebbles, scattering them.

A low growl up ahead pulled Kia out of her thoughts. A dog standing by an overturned garbage can barked at them. Damon pulled Kia to a stop. He glared at the dog. "Go," Damon said quietly.

The dog stopped barking. It lowered its head and its ears flattened. It whined and whimpered, then turned and ran away.

"I'm not much of a dog lover," Damon said, walking again.

Rats he was okay with; dogs he didn't like. She felt a quick chill.

They reached the edge of the park and Damon looked down at her. "I'll take you to your place, but I won't come up. Okay?"

Kia gazed up at him, her face relaxing. A smile of understanding replaced her worried, pursed lips. He wasn't mad—he was controlling himself. Should she tell him anything he wanted to do was all right with her? Then she remembered that she couldn't invite him upstairs.

"Okay," she said.

They strolled along the empty streets, Damon joking about the rich people who lived in the neighborhood, talking about music, telling her things about the city she didn't know—about the subway station that was never completed years and years ago but was still there like an underground ghost town, about colonial days, about places on the Lower East

Side that had been notorious in the nineteenth century. She didn't pay much attention; she couldn't. She was too aware of him, too alive to his presence to be able to hear anything other than the sound of his voice. She did wonder how he knew so much history, about things that took place so long ago, how old he really was, where he had come from—but then she caught sight of his sharp cheekbone, the lips that had been on her mouth, and she lost the thread of the thought.

They arrived on her corner. "Better that we're not seen together," she said. "My building is just up the street."

Damon nodded, his dark eyes narrowing as he studied her face. "I won't ask you any questions," he said. "I don't need to know."

Kia tipped up her face, expecting him to kiss her; instead he just pressed his lips against her forehead and stepped back. "Good night."

Disappointed, Kia looked down at the ground. "Good night," she said.

He pulled something from his pocket and held it out to her. She took it and saw that it was a flyer for another "invitation only" event.

"Maybe I'll see you there," he said.

Kia looked up at him. "Maybe." So he still invited her even though she hadn't worked up the nerve to go to the last one. She cleared her throat. "Thank you. For tonight."

He gave her a little bow. "My pleasure. Really." He grinned. "Well, I hope there was some pleasure for you too."

Kia laughed. "Oh yeah."

"Good. And now, before you tempt me any further, I'm going to take off."

"See you."

She watched him step off the curb and flag a cab. Once he was out of sight, she let out a little shriek and collapsed onto a stone planter in a fit of giggles.

The doorman came out of her building. He glanced up and down the street, spotted her, then stood there. Watching. Kia headed inside.

She shut her eyes in the elevator, leaning against the wall as she rode up to her floor, remembering how it felt to be so close to Damon, to have him caress her skin, to press against him with abandon.

Then she remembered the rats and felt that same chill again.

The elevator stopped and she pulled out her keys. Slipping inside the apartment, she realized there had been all kinds of strange moments: Rex and then that girl, the rats, the dog. Even the turtles hurling themselves into the water. Everything seemed to react to something about Damon.

Then she remembered something else. When they stopped making out, when he pulled away and decided it was time to go.

What had he meant about that being a bad a idea? Why would he think that?

Her shoulders slumped. Maybe Kali really was his girlfriend and he didn't want to cheat on her.

Or maybe . . . A tiny current ran through her, making her skin tingle.

What if all those odd occurrences pointed to something about Damon that Kia hadn't let herself really believe? An explanation right in front of her—hiding in plain sight.

What if the most logical explanation that tied together

everything she had discovered about him was also the most impossible?

Kia finally let the thought reveal itself bare and unadorned: Damon was a real vampire. And he wanted to stop because he was he worried he would get carried away and bite her for real.

Kia sat on her bed and gazed at her reflection in her mirror.

Would I stop him?

ELEVEN

What does siring mean?" Kia asked Hecate during work the next afternoon.

Hecate looked up from the pile of shoes she was sorting. A bunch of girls had tried on almost every shoe in the store and now Hecate and Kia were putting them all back.

"Siring?" Hecate repeated. "In vampire terms, you mean?"

"Yeah." Kia stacked a box on top of the pile. "This weird guy, Rex Notorious, said something about siring to Damon last night."

Kia had already given Hecate most of the details of her incredible night.

Hecate snorted. "Rex is whack. Don't pay attention to him."

"I'm not," Kia assured her. "But he said some strange things that I didn't understand." She sighed. "I just don't want to seem stupid or naive or something around Damon."

Hecate paired some stray shoes and stuck them in their

boxes. "Siring is what it's called when you make someone a vampire. At least, according to the lore."

Kia stared at the boots in her hands. Rex had thought that Damon was her sire. That he had made her into a vampire.

She frowned. "So then, what's blood-bonding?" she asked.

"I'm not sure," Hecate said. "I think it's how vampires get married. They drink each other's blood and then they're bonded for life. Or afterlife." She laughed at her own joke.

"Hmm."

Hecate's almond eyes widened. "Did Damon suggest you two get blood-bonded?"

"I wish." Kia sighed. "I think he and Kali might be blood-bonded."

"Oh." Hecate frowned. "That's like going after someone who's married, Kia."

"Yeah." She felt deflated. "But if he was really serious about her, he wouldn't be with me. He seems pretty unhappy. In fact, the reason we went uptown was because he said he was sick of all those people."

"Maybe he does need a change. But seriously, Kia, he's gotta be a lot older than you. I know he's deeply hot, and you like him, but be careful."

"Of what?"

"I don't know. Just . . . be careful is all." Hecate started shelving boxes. "Damon and Kali, well, like I said, they're into a much more intense scene. I just like to play around with the vampire thing. I don't take it all that seriously. Plain old goth works for me too."

"Oh." Kia glanced at Hecate. What if she could show her

what it was really like with Damon? Maybe then she'd understand.

"Listen, I know it isn't exactly your scene," Kia said, getting up and grabbing her purse, "but do you want to go with
me to this?" She handed Hecate the flyer Damon had given
her.

Hecate let out a low whistle. "Interesting."

"Damon gave it to me last night," Kia said, feeling warm at
the memory.

Hecate cocked her head, the beads in her braids clinking
against each other. "Are you sure he'd want you to bring me
along? Third wheel, you know."

"I don't think he'd mind," Kia said. "It's a party. Not a real
date date." What she didn't say was that going on her own made
her nervous—she was afraid she wouldn't know how to act or
that she'd get there and Damon would be busy with Kali.

"I have to say, I am intrigued," Hecate admitted, rocking
back on her heels. "I've heard rumors. . . ."

"Like what?" Kia asked, eager for any information she could
gather.

Hecate shrugged and handed Kia back the invitation. "Just
that it can get really intense. That it's the true inner sanctum."

Kia looked down at the flyer. If going to this party brought
her deeper into Damon's world, then she wanted to be there.
"So, you're in?" she asked Hecate.

Hecate nodded slowly. "I'm in."

The address on the invitation wasn't very far from Vampyre
Central. With the entire stock of NightTimes at their disposal,

Hecate and Kia were outfitted spectacularly. They were determined to fit in, so they really did it up.

Hecate had chosen a skirt that was no more than strips of leather studded onto a wide sash. She wore it over a fishnet body stocking and tall boots. With Hecate's petite figure, big eyes, and glitter makeup she looked like an S-and-M version of one of Shakespeare's fairies.

Kia stuck with the Victorian style that had become her trademark, tweaked by Hecate. She wore a corset made of shiny black leather. It was designed to leave gaps between the lacings, so she had a lot of exposed skin, which she covered with glittering body lotion. Her skirt hung low on her hips and was long in back but short in the front, so that she flashed the tops of her thigh-high stockings when she took long strides. A studded leather choker completed the look. She and Hecate both "borrowed" warm, floor-length velvet cloaks.

"This isn't a club," Hecate said when they arrived at the address on the flyer. "This is an apartment building."

"Well, it's a party," Kia said. "Makes sense that it would be at someone's house."

"It also means that all bets are off in terms of rules."

"Oh." Kia felt a twinge of apprehension.

A muscular bald man with an intricate tattoo covering one side of his face answered the door. "Invitation?" he growled.

Kia held up the flyer. "Damon gave it to me," she added.

The bouncer eyed her, then Hecate. Kia bristled under his scrutiny. After a long moment, the man stood aside and the girls entered the building. "Loft three," he called after them. "Take the elevator."

Usually Kia had to work to keep up with petite Hecate, but now she led the way. She pushed the button, then she pushed it three more times.

"A little eager?" Hecate teased.

Kia blushed. "I should play it more cool, shouldn't I?"

Hecate laughed. "Just a bit."

The elevator arrived and a bare-chested man in leather pants stood in the entrance. "Where are you going?" he asked.

"Loft three," Kia said, trying to sound confident and not look at his nipple rings.

"Invitation?" he demanded.

"Wow, serious security here," Hecate murmured as Kia showed the invitation again. "This is way beyond velvet ropes."

The half-naked guy pressed a button and the elevator took them up to the third floor, then opened directly into the loft. They were in.

Stepping off the elevator, the first thing Kia noticed was the smell. Pungent incense made the room smoky, and it tickled the back of Kia's throat. The space was very dark, illuminated only by candles. It took a moment for Kia's eyes to adjust from the bright fluorescent light in the elevator. Once the bodies and furniture became distinct from one another, her heart thudded harder.

"Now I get it," Hecate said beside her. "All the screening. This is one high-intensity event."

"Yeah," Kia said, her breath long and slow. "And we've been invited in."

They hung their cloaks on a rack, then stepped farther away from the elevator. The room was large and obviously formerly some kind of industrial space. It had exposed brick walls and pipes everywhere and all the windows were painted black. There were several low sofas in the center of the room, and lying on the large coffee table was a woman in a corset, a torn white lace skirt pushed up around her waist, revealing a garter belt and stockings. People placed bottles, drinks, ashtrays all around her. A few stroked her, while someone helped her drink from a bottle of absinthe. A man dripped wax from one of the many candles onto her exposed thigh; she never flinched.

Music thrummed at a low decibel, more a feeling than a sound. Kia heard laughing and sighing, and nearby someone was humming, but it wasn't the same tune that was playing over the loudspeakers.

"This is kinda weird," Hecate said. "See anyone you know?"

A couple crouched in the corner, snorting some kind of powder. Glasses of dark red liquid were perched everywhere. Kia peered into the shadows, wanting a drink badly. And even more badly, she wanted to find Damon.

She heard applause in the next room. "There must be some kind of performance going on in there," she said to Hecate. "Let's check it out."

"Okay," Hecate said. They wound their way through the couples, trios, and foursomes making out and stepped through a brick archway.

"Oh my God," Hecate gasped beside Kia.

Kia's mouth dropped open. This room was even larger, large enough to have a rickety wooden platform set up at one end of it as a stage. Onstage, handcuffed to wall pipes, were a man and a woman. Both were naked to the waist; the man wore only a leather thong, the woman the same. The woman faced the room; the man had his back to the crowd.

What held Kia riveted was the blood. She moved straight through the crowd to the front, forgetting Hecate, pulled by the sight.

Thin red lines crisscrossed the pair's bodies. The man had scarring all along his back, and Kia realized they must be from much older, deeper cuts. They created an intricate pattern on either side of his spine. Fresh cuts bled in diagonal stripes. The woman had her head thrown back against the pipe and Kia could see a long, winding cut from just under her jawline, down between her collarbones, and ending just above her bare nipple. She too had the faint lines of previous cuts. Two men wielding scalpels stood on either side of the stage. They wore little vials of red liquid around their necks.

Kia felt a hand on her arm. "Come on, let's go. This is way over my limit," Hecate said, tugging slightly.

Kia let Hecate lead her away from the edge of the stage. As they left the performance area and went back into the front room, Kia's eyes landed on Damon.

He leaned against a blacked-out window, two women slumped at his feet, a man gazing up adoringly at him. What struck Kia was how bored Damon looked.

Until he saw her.

He smiled and stepped over the women.

"You came," he said, his smile brightening the entire corner of the dark room, the entire world.

"Yeah, but we're leaving," Hecate said.

"Oh?" Damon looked at Kia, his pale eyebrows arched above his black eyes.

Kia shook Hecate's hand off her arm. "I'm not."

"Kia?" Hecate looked around the room, then at Damon. "Are you sure?"

Kia nodded. "Go ahead. I'll be fine."

"I hope you know what you're doing," Hecate said. "But if this is your scene, who am I to kill the buzz, right?"

"Right," Damon answered for Kia.

Hecate walked away and the room blurred around Kia; all she could see was Damon. She knew that all kinds of kinky weirdness was taking place around her, that the drinks might be drugged, that it had become something of a clothing-optional event, but she didn't care. Damon had his hand on her hip as if it belonged there by right, as if she was his. Just how she wished it.

"So I guess you made it upstairs all right the other night," he said.

Kia nodded.

"That was fun going uptown," he said, moving her hair away from her neck. "It was like visiting a foreign country without the jet lag."

"And no bags to lug around," Kia said, feeling his fingers on her flesh and surprised that she could speak at all.

"What do you think of the party?" he asked, studying her face.

"I haven't decided yet," she said carefully.

"Ahhh, taking a wait-and-see attitude."

"I guess."

"Want a drink? Wine? Bloodbath?"

Remembering that Damon didn't drink, she shook her head no. Besides, she already felt intoxicated.

"Just blood, right?" he joked. "Typical purist vampire."

Startled, she laughed. "I guess," she said, covering.

Damon slipped his arm across her shoulders and Kia wondered where Kali was.

"The fangs are out in full force tonight," Damon said.

Kia looked around. He was right. In the clubs the fang wearers were in the minority, but here almost everyone had fangs. Everyone but her—and Damon. She thought of the cutting in the other room. Were people going to start using their teeth instead of scalpels?

She shivered. That was too much for her to accept.

"Lots of action tonight," Damon said, watching a woman being nuzzled by two men on either side of her throat and a woman sucking on her wrist.

Kia's stomach knotted as she wondered what Damon might expect her to be okay with—and she wondered what she might find herself willing to do.

More applause came from the other room. Kia's head whipped toward the archway; she was curious what might be happening.

"Shall we?" Damon said, his full lips sneaking up into a smile.

"Sure." With Damon's hands guiding her through the room, Kia felt she could handle anything. Or would at least force herself to try.

There were more people in the performance room. The man and woman were still handcuffed, and new tracks of blood trickled along their exposed skin.

Damon licked his lips.

Once again, Kia became aware of other people noticing her with Damon. It made her feel proud, like a chosen one.

"Is this your place?" Kia asked.

Damon's eyes stayed on the man and woman on the stage. He didn't seem to have heard her.

"Do you live here?" Kia tried again. She desperately wanted to know more about him.

"What?" Damon leaned his head toward her so he could hear her without taking his eyes off the stage. The music wasn't very loud, so Kia knew the reason he wasn't hearing her was because he was too fascinated by what he was watching.

He took a few steps toward the stage, moving away from Kia. She scurried to stay with him. He didn't seem to notice. It was as if he was being pulled up there. Compelled by something.

The blood.

She reached for his hand, but he moved too quickly. He pushed his way through the crowd and leapt up onto the stage.

He turned to face them and grinned.

Fangs.

He had fangs.

She blinked. *He didn't have them a minute ago. He's never had them before.*

She'd never seen him around blood before.

He turned his back on the crowd again—and sank his teeth into the woman's neck.

The crowd went wild.

He's not doing that, Kia thought. *He's not.*

The woman let out a shriek and went limp. If she weren't

handcuffed, she would have slumped to the floor. Damon ran his hand along her bare breasts, up and down her body, smearing the blood that had risen from the earlier cutting.

Kali appeared—once again in all white—and pulled Damon from the woman. With all the smeared blood, Kia couldn't tell if Damon had actually bitten the woman. Her neck was intensely red, but it could have been blood from the cuts or . . .

Or he could have used his vampire fangs to feed on her.

The crowd was clapping rhythmically, pounding glasses and their feet. "Drain her!" someone shouted. "Drink it all!" another cried.

Damon faced the crowd with blood on his face, shut his eyes, and smiled. He seemed to be drinking in the chants, the cheers. Kali stared at the crowd a moment, then pulled Damon offstage.

The cutting ritual began again.

Kia stumbled backward until she could lean against a wall. She rubbed her palms against the rough concrete behind her, their solid reality welcome in the murky, unchartered surroundings. She needed to ground herself or she'd be washed away into something she didn't understand.

What did I just see?

"You were with Damon," said a man next to her wearing a leather vest and leather pants. He looked about thirty and had long thick curls and dark blue tattoos on his bare arms.

Kia nodded.

The man stepped in front of her and placed his hands on the wall behind her, trapping her. "Has he made you already?"

"He's waiting for me," Kia responded, not understanding the question. "I should go find—"

The man grabbed Kia's wrists and pressed them against the wall. He leaned in close, looking up and down at her body, his gaze resting a long time at her cleavage, then finally he seemed to fixate on her neck. "If he hasn't made you, I'd be happy to be your sire."

That word again.

"You can't," Damon's voice cut in. "Posers and users can't sire."

The guy glanced over his shoulder to see who had interrupted. When he realized it was Damon, he released Kia's wrists. He turned to face Damon but still blocked Kia.

"Hey, Damon, just checking out the new girl," he said. "No offense."

"Get out of her personal space, Void," Damon ordered.

"I've never seen you so territorial," Void said, a smirk on his face. "Interesting. If you don't want to share, maybe—"

"I mean it, Void. Move. Now."

Void looked startled by the ferocity in Damon's voice. He shook his head and walked away.

"You okay?" Damon asked.

Kia stared at him. The blood was gone. So were the fangs. Had she imagined it?

No. She knew what she saw. She didn't make that up.

"Kia?"

Kia realized she hadn't answered him "Yeah, I'm okay. Thanks."

Now Kali came over. She nodded at Kia, clearly recognizing her. Kia stiffened—was Kali going to take Damon away from her?

"We need your expertise," Kali said to Damon in her low, throaty voice. "Let's get this party into gear."

"Right," Damon said, breaking away from Kia to focus on Kali. "Be there in a sec."

Kali took a step away but hovered nearby, watching.

She's jealous, Kia thought, the realization filling her with something like glee.

Damon looked at Kia again. "Gotta spin some discs," he told her.

"Okay," Kia said.

"Don't worry about Void," he added. "I think I was pretty clear that you're off-limits."

Kia nodded. It was beginning to sink in that Damon had defended her honor—had stepped in to keep some guy from . . . what? From *siring* her. The thought that Damon might feel possessive about her thrilled her. She had started to reach up to kiss him when she glimpsed Kali over his shoulder. Not knowing the full story between Damon and Kali made her self-conscious. Kia dropped her hands and mumbled, "Thanks."

"Later," he said. He backed away, then turned and joined Kali. They went to a console in the corner. Damon knelt down and began flipping through CDs and LPs.

Kia stood and watched him, his elegant hands, his lithe, catlike movements. Kali glanced at her and Kia shifted her eyes back up to the stage again; she didn't want Kali to catch her staring at Damon like a swoony, moonstruck kid.

The man and woman handcuffed to the pipes were being released from their restraints. The blood had dried in intricate patterns on their bodies, like tattoos. A woman carrying a whip took their place.

Kia went back into the front room. She spotted Void by the

windows, talking to a woman caressing a snake. It slithered across her shoulders and flicked its tongue at Kia as she walked by. Void and the snake woman both stared at her as she passed. She knew they were talking about her.

She straightened her shoulders and jutted out her jaw. She could feel other eyes on her, and she was sure it was because of Damon. They knew she was special. Because of him.

Kia found a wall to lean against. Everywhere she looked, there were groups in weird configurations; she didn't want to observe anyone too closely.

Suddenly she wished Hecate hadn't gone home. She looked down at the ground to avoid seeing a completely naked guy tracing his veins with a scalpel. She could see why this would be too much.

"Hey." A woman in full vampire drag—dyed black hair, powdered white skin, red contact lenses, and fangs and wearing nothing but a black lace body stocking with lace-up thigh-high boots—stepped in front of Kia.

Kia stepped back. "Hey," she said cautiously.

"Gorgeous corset," the woman said.

"Thanks."

"You work at NightTimes, don't you?" the woman asked.

"Yes."

"I thought I'd seen you there. I'm Lady Margaritte, House of Draconia."

"Kia."

"This is a little too much for you, isn't it?" Lady Margaritte said, as if reading her thoughts.

Kia shrugged. She didn't want it getting back to Damon that she couldn't handle the scene. *His* scene.

"It was like that for me too the first few times. The *public* aspect," Lady Margaritte said. "People doing things at a party most people barely admit doing behind closed doors."

Like me and cutting, Kia thought with a sudden rush of fear.

"Don't worry, it's all about consent here. And there are plenty of us who just watch."

"It's cool," Kia said. Lady Margaritte seemed nice enough; she was certainly trying to make Kia feel comfortable. But what she didn't understand was that Damon was the only reason she was there.

"You are vampire," Lady Margaritte said. "I can see that. Damon saw that too. We've noticed how he singles you out."

Kia smiled. So that's why this woman was talking to her.

"Are you aligned?" Lady Margaritte asked.

Kia figured that since she didn't know what that meant, she probably wasn't. "No," she said.

Lady Margaritte smiled too. "You should come to court. Damon is obviously your protector, but it's best to be aligned with a house."

"Is Damon with your house?" Kia asked.

"Damon is council," Lady Margaritte said. She seemed surprised that Kia didn't know this. "So he can't be aligned with one house."

"Right, of course," Kia bluffed. The vampire community was more complex than she had realized.

"House of Draconia, next week at Red," Lady Margaritte said. "Do you know it?"

Kia nodded. Red was a bar a few blocks away from NightTimes. "Maybe I'll see you there," Kia said.

"You would be most welcome." Lady Margaritte gave a slight bow and moved away.

Kia heard someone shriek in the performance room, then applause. The shrieks continued, sending chills along Kia's flesh. She didn't want to know what was going on in there. She pushed away the thought that Damon was somehow involved, grabbed her cloak, and left the party.

The bouncer in the elevator ignored her and they rode down together in silence. Kia stepped out onto a deserted street. The cold, brisk wind made her shiver, but she knew the shakiness in her legs was because the scene in that loft had been a lot more disconcerting than she had let herself admit.

If Carol and Aaron had seen those people, what they were doing— She shook her head and forced the idea out of her mind.

And Damon. What really happened up there? Did the blood and the cutting excite him so much that he couldn't help revealing his vampire side?

She charged down the steps into the subway, her mind filled with the image of the man and the woman being cut.

She paced the platform, unable to stand still, and when the empty subway train arrived, she couldn't sit down either.

Maybe that's the pull, she thought. *The reason cutting is so tempting, why Damon has chosen me.* Maybe she was tapping into some deep vampire quality of her own.

TWELVE

Kia. Come in here, please. I need to talk to you."

Kia froze in the hallway between the living room and her room. Her father sounded serious.

The past week flashed through Kia's mind. She slowly turned and walked down the hall to the living room, flipping through possible errors. Her dad had been back from D.C. so she had been more careful, despite how desperately she had wanted to see Damon since the party. She stepped into the living room warily.

"Kia, there's something we need to talk about." He stood at his desk as if he had just hung up the phone.

She sat on the couch and prepped an "I swear I'll do better, thanks for caring" speech and braced herself for whatever was coming.

"I'm going over to the hospital," her dad said, leaning against the desk.

Kia's heart clanged against her ribs. If her father was going to see her mom, Kia was in even bigger trouble than she had thought.

"I know you've been busy with school and work," he continued. "So you haven't been there recently."

Was he trying to guilt her? Him? Guilt *her*?

"So you probably don't know that she's being released."

Kia's mouth dropped open. *What did he just say?* "You mean . . . you mean she's cured?" Her voice didn't sound like her own. She sounded about ten years old. "She's all better now?"

Her dad took off his glasses. He rubbed them with the end of his shirt for a few minutes. Kia was struck suddenly that his eyes were the same color as hers.

He put his glasses back on. "Not exactly," he said. He looked down at his hands. The white patch where his wedding ring used to be had long since faded and become tanned like the rest of his hand.

"Wh-what do you mean?" Kia asked.

"They can't keep her in the hospital anymore. They've done their treatments and the surgery and now they're sending her home to see how things go."

"Oh." Kia nodded. She nodded again. "So I should pack?"

"Well, no." Her dad stood up and shoved his hands in his pockets. "The treatments . . . you know how they wipe her out. You're going to stay on here."

"Till she's better," Kia said.

"She has daily health aides to help her, and Maggie is going to stay with her."

"Maggie?" Kia asked. Maggie was a longtime friend of her

mom's. When Kia was little, she had thought they were related. "Why not me?"

"Your mom is still really sick," her dad said. "And weak. She—we think it would be better for you to just stay here. You know, be a kid. She doesn't want you to have to take care of her. You've got your own stuff. School. Friends." Her dad smiled. "Boys," he added in a teasing voice.

Yeah, right, Dad. I need to have time to think about hanging at ye olde soda shoppe with "boys."

"So this is what Mom wants?" Kia asked. She realized *that* was what actually mattered here.

Her dad nodded. "It's how she wants it. How we both want it."

"This is good news, right?" Kia asked. "They wouldn't send her home unless they thought she was getting better."

Now he sighed. "I won't lie to you, Kia. I just don't know. I think they want to see if the treatments worked this time."

Kia pressed against the back of the sofa, her feet hard and solid on the floor. She felt light-headed, as if her brain were a balloon trying to float away.

"So, we'll see how everything goes," her dad said. He gave her a big, fake smile. "Things are going well here, don't you think? I'm not such a bad roomie."

Kia stared at him and then made the edges of her mouth curve up. "Sure thing. You up for a pillow fight? *Roomie?*"

Her dad laughed. He obviously didn't hear the acid dripping from her voice.

"Maybe another time." He stood and stretched, as if the conversation had tightened all his muscles. "So, I'm going to take off. Are you working at the store today?"

"Yeah, the late shift," Kia said. "Since it's Saturday." She wasn't actually scheduled, but it gave her an excuse to get out of the house.

"Well, take a cab home, all right? I worry about you on the subways after eleven."

He patted himself down for his glasses and wallet, grabbed his coat, and left.

Kia stared out the window. *Mom is going home.* That had to be good.

Greta, the other NightTimes employee, was at the cash register when Kia came in later. "Are you on tonight?" she asked, surprised.

Greta was in her thirties and also into the vampire club scene. So into it, in fact, that she wore her fangs at the store, and her talon-like fingernails often interfered with her ability to do many of her tasks. Kia didn't mind. Greta seemed to look up to her. Probably because of Damon.

"Nah," Kia replied. "But I figured I'd stop in. Say hi." She looked around the store. "Is Hecate around?"

Greta nodded toward the storage room. "In the back. Oh, your friend Virgil stopped by earlier."

"Yeah?" Kia said, feigning interest.

Kia went into the storeroom, where Hecate was making a list on a notepad. She glanced up when she heard Kia come in.

"Hi, what's up?" Hecate asked.

"My mom's going home," Kia blurted. "That's good, right?"

"Wow," Hecate said. "Yeah, that's good." Her brow furrowed. "I think."

"It was good when your gramps got released," Kia pressed.

Hecate nodded. "Definitely."

"They wouldn't boot her out of a hospital if she was still really sick, would they?"

Hecate shrugged. "I don't think so."

Kia sat on a box. "That's what I think too."

"So does that mean you're leaving rich papa uptown?"

"Nah," Kia said. "He said my mom is still too weak to have me there. I'll probably move back in sometime soon, though."

"That'll be cool. Though your mom is more likely to keep closer tabs on you than your dad. That'll cut down on some of what you're doing."

Kia sat up straighter. "You're right. I've been able to see Damon because Dad is out of town so much."

Hecate bit her lip as if she were deciding something. "Kia," she said slowly. "You're not exactly seeing him. Not in a boyfriend-girlfriend way."

Kia stared at Hecate. "I know. But he does think I'm special. Every time I go to a club where he is, he pays a lot of attention to me. He's even kissed me. In front of Kali."

"Great guy," Hecate muttered.

Kia stood up. "You don't know him. Not like I do."

"You don't really know him either," Hecate said.

"I know more than you think," Kia replied. *Like the fact that he might actually be a vampire.* Even just letting the thought run through her mind gave her an icy chill, the same one she felt whenever she wondered if it could really, possibly be true.

"Was that party what you expected?" Hecate asked. "That was way wiggy. And it was Damon's scene. Did you know *that* side of him?"

Kia's jaw tensed. Yes, it did kind of shock her to see Damon at the center of such a wild event. Funny. That party freaked her out more than the idea that he might be an actual vampire.

"I was okay with it," Kia said. "I'm sorry I brought you there since you weren't."

Hecate frowned.

She's turning into another Carol, Kia thought.

"Hey, don't get pissed," Hecate said. She shrugged. "If that's what you're into, that's what you're into. I just think the Damon thing has danger zone all over it."

"You're wrong," Kia said.

"Here's hoping," Hecate said. Then she grinned. "So, spill. What kind of kisser is he? Insistent and eager? Forceful and strong? Gentle and soulful?"

Kia giggled. "All of the above. And more."

"Way to go, girlfriend." Hecate smirked. "Mmm. I need to get some action soon."

"You could have had plenty at that party," Kia teased. "Too bad you left."

"I like my action blood-free, thanks. Saves on the dry cleaning."

"Got a point." Kia felt better now that they were joking about this stuff. Still, she knew she'd have to tone down some of what she told Hecate.

Back to having secrets, she thought.

Greta appeared in the door of the stockroom. "Hecate, can you ring up a customer?"

Hecate rolled her eyes. "You've got to cut your nails, Gret. They've become a workplace liability."

"But they're finally looking lethal," Greta objected. "It took a long time and a lot of care to grow them."

"Whatever."

Kia followed Hecate and Greta into the store. Julie stood at the cash register.

"Hey, Kia, are you going to Crash tonight?" Julie asked.

Crash was a regular goth club on the West Side, though vampires sometimes hung out there too—without their fangs.

"Probably," Kia said. After all, her father thought she was working. And Damon was DJ-ing.

"Cool. Then I'll go too." Julie took her bag and left. Almost immediately, the door chimes rang and Aaron walked in.

Kia stared. What was he doing here?

Looking completely out of place among the leather, velvet, and rubber in his khakis and L.L. Bean jacket, he strode straight over to Kia. He looked upset.

Kia had avoided Carol and Aaron at school all week. After her meltdown during their stupid spell night last weekend she couldn't bring herself to look at them—much less talk. Just seeing them reminded her of her humiliating crack-up.

But now Aaron was practically hyperventilating in front of her.

"I'm really glad you're here," he said. He spoke rapidly, as if the words were being thrust out of his mouth. "Can we—can we talk somewhere private?" he asked.

It occurred to Kia that Aaron might be worried about her, might be reaching out.

"Sure. I'm not actually working today." Kia led him to the storeroom, wondering if she could handle the conversation they were about to have.

Still, she thought, flipping a carton over to sit on, it was because she fell apart that she and Damon had wound up together in Central Park. *Maybe I ought to be thanking Carol and Aaron instead of being pissed at how far they pushed me.* Why should she care if they were into that silly Wicca stuff and not into the vampire thing? She preferred keeping Damon and that world all to herself anyway.

"Michael dumped me," Aaron blurted.

"Oh." Kia blinked a few times, trying to grasp the fact that Aaron was here to talk about something entirely different than she had expected.

Aaron paced the small room. "Out of the blue. For no apparent reason."

"Wow." Her head whirled as she played mental catch-up. So, apparently he *wasn't* at all worried about her since the last time he'd seen her, when she'd been a complete wreck?

"I thought we were getting on fine," he continued. "He actually seemed to like me. I liked him." He covered his face in his hands. "I must have come on too strong. Too . . . needy. Scared him away. Maybe I can get him back. Tell him I didn't mean all those things. Make him think I don't like him at all. That should help, right? But why would liking someone less make them like me more? It makes no sense. Oh, man. What do you think, can get him back? Kia?"

Kia opened her mouth, closed it. She had been a blubbering mess of tears, snot, and gulping sobs on his floor last week. *Michael. Elf Boy.* She was really struggling to focus.

"Kia?" Aaron repeated, his forehead wrinkling.

"Sure," she said.

"Are you even paying attention?" he snapped. "It's like I'm talking to a brick wall."

Kia bristled. "Sorry I can't get all misty over your love life," she said. "I've got problems of my own."

Aaron stared back at her. "You know, I realize that your mom is sick and that's hell," he began, "but you don't have a monopoly on problems. We've given you a lot of space, a lot of slack for not being so on top of the whole 'best friend' thing lately. But I think you might want to remember that it goes both ways—we're going through stuff too, you know."

Kia's jaw tightened. Typical. Define her solely as the kid with the sick mom.

"What happened to you, Kia? You used to give a shit."

Kia's eyes narrowed as he continued his tirade.

"Do you even care what is going on with Carol?" he demanded, his voice growing louder, his face red. "Her brother has completely vanished—not a word for weeks. She's sad all the time now."

"Gee. I guess your little magic spells didn't work," Kia said. The cold words spilled out before she'd even really thought them while a mixture of emotions fought inside her—worry for Carol, sympathy for what Aaron was going through, anger and frustration that they were all so far apart now and none of them could help each other if they tried. "I guess you're discovering that there's a big difference between playing kiddie games and being the real deal. So grow up and get over it," she finished.

Aaron stared at her for a long moment, shook his head, and walked out.

Kia pressed her lips together, fighing a queasy feeling in her stomach, the flush creeping across her face.

She stalked to a rack and yanked the hangers, pawing the new corsets. She was going to treat herself to a brand-new outfit. Screw Aaron and Carol. Tonight at Crash she was going to begin her quest.

She was going to uncover Damon's real identity.

THIRTEEN

Pounding music blasted as Kia strolled past the bouncer at Crash later that night. She never paid a cover anymore, never worried about getting in.

The club was bigger than it looked on the outside, with three bars and a stage at the far end. Girls danced in cages on either side of the stage, and another three danced on the bars.

Mixed crowd, she observed. She recognized vamps from other clubs scattered throughout, along with a large contingency of goth followers. Some faces she thought she remembered from the private event at the loft, but she avoided them. Without Damon by her side, those people made her nervous.

She ordered a bloodbath, which the bartender didn't charge her for, and moved through the club, searching for Damon.

So far, ever since that amazing, magical night in Central Park almost two weeks ago, they hadn't seen each other anywhere but in clubs. Was he avoiding her on purpose? Did he not want to be alone with her?

Maybe she was the wrong kind of temptation.

She watched the girls on the stage gyrate in their corsets, garter belts, and stockings, their high-heel shoes looking lethal. Her eyes traveled from the stage around the club, searching for the DJ booth.

It wasn't up front, so she turned and scanned the balcony.

Fair hair bobbed behind a large speaker. *Gotcha.*

"Kia!"

Kia turned and saw Virgil pushing his way through the crowd to her. "I was wondering if I'd run into you here."

"I heard you were at NightTimes today," Kia said.

Virgil ducked his head, letting his hair cover his face. "I was in the nabe, you know."

"Right." She took a swig of her drink. "Listen, there's someone I need to say hi to."

"Oh. Okay." Virgil looked disappointed. Then he smiled, his dimples on parade. "Later, right?"

"Sure." Kia wandered the club, trying to find the way up to the balcony level, where Damon was. She wandered to the edge of the dance floor and went through a door that opened onto a stairway.

She came out at the balcony, just as she hoped. And even better, Damon was alone. His back was to her as he watched over the console. He was wearing headphones and bouncing a little with the music.

She came up behind him quietly and slipped her hands around him. Startled, he grabbed her hands and yanked her around in front of him. She stumbled, but he caught her by the elbow before she crashed into the mixing board.

"Oh, hey, Kia. Sorry."

"Th-that's okay." She pushed her hair out of her face.

"Reflex," he said. "I don't like being ambushed."

"I didn't mean to startle you," Kia said. "I just . . ." She tried to think of something that would bring his flirtatious charm back. "I just couldn't resist touching you."

He smiled. Good. She fixed it.

"Nothing wrong with that," he said. He leaned against the balcony railing.

Kia stepped toward him until she was so close that her breasts brushed against his chest. She didn't touch him, though. She waited for him to make the next move.

He did.

He gripped her hips and pulled her into him, thrusting his tongue into her mouth with a ferocity that nearly buckled her knees. He felt hungry. Hungry for her.

Kia matched him in intensity, letting her tongue, her hands, her hips all tell him she was his. That she would give him anything he wanted. Anything at all.

His skin is cold, she realized as she kissed his neck. She leaned away from him a moment to push her hair out of her face and noticed again how pale he was. As if he'd never seen daylight.

As if he couldn't.

He grabbed her hair and yanked back her head, exposing her throat.

"Do it," she whispered so quietly she knew that he couldn't hear her, that her words just sounded like breathing.

He hovered above her neck, one hand tangled in her hair, the other stroking her body. He smiled down at her as his hand moved between her thighs. "There are a lot of fake vampires down there wanting to have the first bite," he said. "What do *you* want?"

She wanted to say "you," but she couldn't speak; she could only moan with growing desire for whatever he was offering her.

Several female voices broke them apart. Kia sat down hard on the floor, unable to keep herself standing. Damon leaned against the balcony railing again. "Hello, ladies."

Kia glanced up to see Kali and two of the dancers standing at the doorway. She wondered how much they had seen. Her eyes flicked to Damon. He seemed completely unfazed by the intrusion or the fact that Kali might have seen them together.

The dancers looked at Kia on the floor, then at Kali. Kali's eyes narrowed a moment, then she seemed to recover. "The performers are going to start in about fifteen minutes," Kali told Damon. "So switch to the transition CD when you see me wave."

"Got it." Damon nodded. "You're looking good up there," he told the dancers. "Let me know if you want me to play you anything special."

"Thanks, Damon," the blond dancer said. "And that CD you made me rocked. Thanks for dropping it off last night."

"Glad you liked it."

Jealousy rippled through Kia's body like a seizure. She wanted to tear the long blond hair from the woman's head and cram it down her throat. Instead she got up and said, "See you later," to Damon and hurried back down the stairs.

She had to show him she didn't care about stuff like that, Kia vowed. Kali could play it cool—so could she.

She exited the stairwell and found Virgil staring up at the dancer wriggling on the bar. "Hey, Virgil," she said. "Wanna dance?"

"Not really," he told her. "I'm more into leaning, actually. Sometimes I do shift from side to side, but that's about the extent of it."

"Oh."

She glanced up to the balcony. She could see Damon's fair hair easily even in the dark room. Could he see her?

"Well, then I'll dance for both of us," she declared. She moved a few feet from the bar, hoping she was visible to the balcony, and danced. If Damon was into those dancer girls, then she'd show him she could move just like them.

Kia flung her hair, wiggled and writhed, twirled, and threw sexy glances at Virgil. Virgil seemed stunned and unsure of how to react. He alternated between staring at her and looking away.

The music ended, and Kia looked up to the balcony. She could no longer see Damon. She returned to Virgil's side.

Lady Margaritte, the woman who had spoken to her at the loft, approached her. "Kia, nice to see you again."

Kia wondered what Virgil thought of Lady Margaritte's fangs and then realized a bigger question would be what he would have thought of that party. It didn't matter. She wasn't looking for his—or anyone else's—approval. Well, no one but Damon's.

"Hi, This is Virgil," Kia said.

"Welcome, Virgil," Lady Margaritte said. "Kia, I hope you'll consider coming to court. Tomorrow at eight."

"I'll think about it."

"Good." She left, and Julie and Mandy appeared. "We're going to split," Julie said.

"You ready to go?" Virgil asked Kia.

Kia looked around for Damon, figuring if there were going to be performances, he'd go on a break and maybe she could get another chance to spend some time alone with him.

Instead she saw him flanked by Kali and the two dancers, chatting at the far end of the bar. Disappointed, she pasted a big smile on her face and slipped her arm into Virgil's. "Sure. Let's get out of here."

Kia paused at the door, holding her keys. It was Sunday, and Kia had decided to see her mom. It was strange to go back home, knowing that she was just visiting. Maggie was living there now, so maybe she should give them some warning before just barging in.

She rang the doorbell.

"Are you expecting someone?" she heard Maggie ask on the other side of the door. Kia didn't hear her mother's response, but a moment later the door opened.

"Kia!" Maggie smiled, creating a mass of wrinkles on her tanned face. Maggie had always looked older than Kia's mom. She'd spent so much time at her beach house that she was a dermatologist's warning poster. She didn't dye her hair either, so it was a mass of white, gray, and dark brown.

"Hi, Maggie," Kia said. "Can I come in?"

"Of course," Maggie said, stepping away from the door. "Your mom will be thrilled to see you." She leaned in to whisper, "I think she's been missing you."

Kia swallowed. There was that little guilt-o-meter again, going off in her chest. "I—I've been busy."

Maggie gave her a sidelong look. "Are you all right? You seem—"

"Hey, that's new." Kia cut her off as she stepped into the small kitchen and noticed a gleaming white microwave. "How'd you get Mom to agree? She always said they were just expensive warmer-uppers." She glanced to where Maggie stood in the doorway. She quickly turned back to the microwave. "Oh," she said, opening and closing the microwave door. "She's on some sort of special diet, right?"

"Something like that," Maggie said.

Kia took a breath and turned. "Well, I see microwave pop-corn in my future."

Maggie grinned at her. "Mine too."

Maggie followed Kia down the hallway. As they passed Kia's room—*My former room,* Kia thought with a twinge—she peeked in. Maggie's clothes were strewn everywhere. There were still reminders of Kia's previous existence in the room, but only a shadow of them.

A sturdy woman with dark skin and big brown eyes came out of Kia's mother's room.

"Lola," Maggie said. "This is Ms. Carruther's daughter, Kia."

"Hello, Kia," Lola replied. She had a strong Jamaican accent.

"Lola is your mom's home health aide," Maggie explained. "She's here a few hours every day."

"Oh," Kia said. She didn't know what else she was supposed to say.

"If you want to go in, she's all cleaned up," Lola said.

What does that mean? Kia wondered, but didn't ask.

"She's pretty weak," Maggie warned. "And she's lost more weight."

More? She didn't have any weight to lose the last time Kia had seen her. Kia braced herself and went into her mother's room.

It was nice to see her mom in her own bed, but the additions to the room were startling. Much more than the microwave in the kitchen or Maggie's invasion. Pill bottles were lined up on the nightstand, and a large bowl sat on a chair beside the bed. The stack of adult diapers on the dresser seriously freaked her out, so she turned so she couldn't see them, concentrating only on her mom.

Maggie was right—her mom was even thinner. Her eyes were enormous in her gaunt face. But at least they were clear and bright.

"Hi, sweetie, what a nice surprise," her mom said. Her voice wasn't any weaker than in the hospital, so that was a relief.

"You're home now," Kia said, unable to think of anything else.

"Big improvement," her mother said. She shut her eyes.

Should I keep talking or does she want to rest?

"How's Carol?" her mother asked, her eyes still closed.

"Uh, fine," Kia replied.

"Her brother?"

"Still AWOL," Kia said. "I think Carol's pretty upset about it."

"Of course." Her mom reached for something on the bed. Kia realized her mom was feeling around for her hand, so she put it within reach. Her mom touched it, then patted it. "It's good that she has you."

Kia swallowed. "Right."

"School?" she asked.

"Okay," Kia replied, falling into her mother's short, clipped sentences.

"Project?"

"Still deciding." Kia hoped her mom wasn't aware how close the end of the semester was. Thanksgiving was fast approaching and the term art project should be well under way by now. Nearly finished, in fact.

"Those charcoals," her mom said. "Good."

"That's an idea," Kia said. She didn't bother explaining the term project was mixed media.

"Mmm." Her mother nodded slightly. Her closed eyelids had tiny blue veins in them. Kia felt as if she could almost see through the thin, translucent skin.

Maggie popped her head into the doorway. "Kia, do you want to stay for lunch?"

"Food." Her mother scowled.

Kia stood up. "Nah," she said.

"It's no bother—I'm just reheating a big pot of stew I made last night."

"I—I've got homework," Kia said.

"Project," her mother said.

"Right, my term art project."

"If you're sure," Maggie said.

Kia nodded and Maggie left the room. Kia heard her clanking around in the small kitchen.

"I'm sorry," her mother said.

Kia's head whipped around from the doorway to her mother on the bed. Her eyes were still closed, as if light hurt them, as if they were vampire eyes.

"Wh-what?" Kia asked.

"Sorry."

Kia's face crumpled. Her breathing tightened and she forced her voice to stay steady. "For what?" she asked, even though she didn't want to know.

"All this," her mother said. "You shouldn't have to . . ." She trailed off.

"It's okay. Really. Everything's cool," Kia said. "Hey, you're back home. Things are going to be better now. No more weird hospital smell. No more doc flocks."

Her mother nodded slowly. She opened her eyes and smiled. "You're a good girl." She shut her eyes again. "I—I'm going to rest now."

"Sure. Sure, Mom." Kia swallowed. She didn't want her mother telling her she was good. She wasn't good. She had hardly been here at all. She had messed up with Carol and Aaron. No, Kia wasn't even a little bit good.

Maggie came out of the kitchen, wiping her hands on a dish towel. "I'll walk you out," she said.

Go away, Kia thought as Maggie put her arm around her waist and gave her a hug.

"You've lost weight too," Maggie commented. "Is your father taking good enough care of you?"

"Sure," Kia said. The weight thing had just seemed to happen—the late hours, the forgetting to eat. Maybe she should write a diet book: *How to Lose Weight the Vampire Way.*

"You know, sometimes your father can be kind of dense," Maggie said. "So if you ever feel the need to talk and don't want to talk to your mom, you can always call me."

The door was in sight, but with Maggie trying to bond, it seemed so far away. "Sure thing," Kia said, trying to take longer strides.

"I'm worried about you, Kia," Maggie said. "Your mother being sick for so long, that's a big deal. Your father——"

"Dad and I are getting along fine," Kia said.

Maggie gave her a sharp look and released her. "I just want you to know you're not alone in this. There are some adults you can count on."

"I know," Kia said reaching for the doorknob. "Thanks." She stepped through the door.

"Welcome to the Court of Draconia, Kia," Lady Margaritte said as Kia walked into Red that night. "I'm glad to see you."

"It sounded interesting," Kia said. "And I want to learn more."

"I'm about to perform our opening ritual," Lady Margaritte said. "Take a seat."

Kia scanned the room for Damon. She didn't see him, but she did spot one of the dancers from the previous night and several other vaguely familiar faces. They nodded at her, obviously recognizing her too.

She sat on a red velvet banquette, wondering what the ritual was going to be. Wondering if she'd be able to handle it.

Lady Margaritte took the stage. She was joined by two other women, both in black vampire gear. One lit incense, the other started beating a small drum. It reminded Kia of the Wicca ritual.

She flashed on Aaron's angry face from the scene in the storeroom the day before. She'd seen him mad in the past but never at her—not like that.

She looked down at her nails and remembered the feel of her mother's thin hand.

So Carol's brother was seriously gone now. Maybe Kia should call her. Or at least e-mail. Of course, by now, Aaron would have told her about their fight, so Kia was probably the last person either of them wanted to hear from.

A gong broke into Kia's thoughts. Lady Margaritte held up a decanter filled with dark, thick liquid.

"The blessing of the blood," she intoned into the microphone.

Kia felt anticipation ripple through the crowd. She wriggled to the edge of her seat.

"Blood is life. Blood is our source. Blood is what binds us to one another. Creatures of the night, bless this blood for us to share, to connect us to the life force, to connect us to one another. What we share, we share willingly."

Kia blinked. Was this a blood-bonding ceremony? She thought that was just between people getting married.

Lady Margaritte waved some smoldering sage around the decanter. Then some other vampires went up onstage and lit candles. They held the candles around the decanter.

"The blood is now purified with sage and with flames. We are free to drink."

Goose bumps rose on Kia's skin.

The vampires began pouring the blood into tiny paper cups that were set up on several trays.

Lady Margaritte smiled at the crowd. "For those who are new to our court, we open with this ceremony to connect with our vampire selves and as a way to acknowledge that despite our many differences, we are linked. This is not a blood-bonding. This is a way to open us up to one another while we're here, to proudly proclaim our vampire nature with each other.

"And," she added with a fanged grin, "for any public health inspectors here undercover, our blood is organic corn syrup mixed with organic food coloring."

Everyone laughed, including Kia.

The vampires worked their way through the crowd, handing out the little cups of fake blood. Once everyone had one, they returned to the stage.

Kia clutched the little cup so tightly she nearly squashed it. She put it down on the table in front of her. A man and a woman, both in their thirties, joined her on the banquette. They smiled at her, their small fangs subtle. Until they each fiddled with the fake teeth, making very un-subtle adjustments, destroying the illusion.

"Now," Lady Margaritte instructed. "Shut your eyes." Kia did. "Pour the blood onto your tongue. Feel its warmth, its vitality. Feel the life force, the life you are part of."

The blood was sweet, not like real blood at all, but Kia concentrated on what Lady Margaritte was saying.

"Now feel it warm your throat, feel it enter your body. Blood is power. You feed on power. This is yours. Own it. You are powerful. You are beautiful. Do not fear your dark self; it is where you draw your strength."

Kia swallowed, unexpected emotions startling her, making her throat close up. *I'm not strong,* flashed through her mind, spreading a potent mix of guilt and grief through her. *I'm not powerful.* If she were, everything would be different. She wouldn't be screwing up everything in her life. She felt tears spring into her eyes, and to her horror, they trickled down her cheeks.

A warm hand covered hers. Her eyes blinked open. "You're okay here," the woman next to her said, her voice soft. "You are safe. No one here will judge you or hurt you."

Kia nodded, her throat clogged.

"We are vampire!" Lady Margaritte declared from the stage.

"We are vampire!" the crowd responded.

A gong sounded and the ritual was over. The woman beside Kia still held her hand. Kia wasn't sure if she should shake it off or not. She was surprised by how calming it felt.

The woman watched her a moment, then smiled. "Rituals call things up in all of us," she said.

Like when I wigged out at Aaron's, Kia remembered.

"We understand," the woman continued. "Your journey is your own. We won't pry. But we are here if you need us." She released Kia's hand.

"Thank you," Kia said.

"I'm Dark Star. This is Osiris."

The man on the woman's other side nodded. He was slight, with narrow shoulders and short light hair. They were both dressed in black, but nothing outrageous. The little fangs and matching pendants were all that said vampire.

"Those are cool," Kia said, pointing at the jewelry.

Dark Star held out the pendant for Kia to look at more closely. It was a pentagram with a vial filled with dark liquid soldered onto the center.

"Osiris and I are blood-bonded," Dark Star explained. "That's what's in the vial."

"Does everyone who blood-bonds wear one of these?" Kia asked.

"Usually," Osiris said. "It's like wearing a wedding band. Making a public commitment."

Damon didn't wear one. Kia's smile broadened.

"You're feeling stronger now?" Dark Star asked.

"Yes," Kia said.

"I'm glad. We need to go, and I'd hate to leave you alone if you were still vulnerable."

"I'm fine now, thanks." Kia was struck by how kind Dark Star was to her—a total stranger. It was like Lady Margaritte said: this ritual made them all part of the same whole.

Kia watched Dark Star and Osiris leave the bar, saying good-bye to several people as they made it to the door.

Where Damon suddenly appeared.

Kia's heart clutched. Was he looking for her? Did he know she was here?

She got up quickly, but everyone was heading for the bar now that the ritual was over and the crowding slowed her down. By the time she got to the door, Damon was gone.

She burst out of the entrance and whipped her head around. A figure with pale hair ducked around a corner a few streets ahead. She raced after him.

"Damon," she called, hurtling around the corner. She skidded to a stop.

The street was empty.

Kia's body sagged with disappointment. There wasn't anything left to do but go home.

FOURTEEN

*T*hank you all for making our court last week such a success. We appreciate
all those who made it possible. And welcome to all our newcomers.
*Remember, if there is anything you have questions about, contact me via this list
and we can set up a private chat.*

   Lady Margaritte

Kia smiled as she read the e-mail. She had signed up for the
Court of Draconia web group and had been checking out the
posts all week. They ranged from practical (*Need a night job to
accommodate my schedule* or *Have a working amp for sale*), to the funny,
to the sad, to the philosophical. There was court business (who
was going to book the club for the next event, when elections
for court officers would be held) and invitations to other vampire nights and band performances. Kia never posted herself;
she felt too new, but she enjoyed reading the varied responses
to what other people wrote.

She tried to figure out if Damon ever posted on the list. One name, NOMAD, appeared occasionally, and the messages sounded like him. But Kia knew enough to know that e-mails could be misleading. She needed proof.

Proof of a lot of things.

"Is he or isn't he?" was the question that woke her up every morning, came to mind whenever she saw him.

At NightTimes she noted that he never came in until well after dark. He was so pale but never wore makeup like the others. His skin was cold to the touch, but he never seemed to notice the temperature. Those rats, the dog, the turtles all acted so strangely in the park, his cryptic statements, his knowledge of things that had happened so long ago, the sudden appearance and disappearance of fangs. The mesmerizing hold he had over her—over everyone who came into contact with him. The power he radiated.

It had to be true.

Am I the only one who knows?

At lunch the following week Kia headed for what had become her usual table over the last two months. Julie, Wren, and Mandy, the center of the goth clique, sat comparing hair dye, jewelry, and bands. Virgil doodled in his sketch pad.

"Hi," Kia said, plopping onto a chair.

Julie, Wren, and Mandy exchanged cryptic glances as if they were telecommunicating. "Hi, Kia," Julie said coolly.

What's with her? Kia wondered.

"So we heard you're seriously into the whole vampire thing," Mandy said.

Kia shot a look at Virgil. He shrugged as if he didn't know what they were talking about.

"We went to a goth club over the weekend," Wren explained.

"Well, that's what we thought." Mandy rolled her eyes.

"It turned out to be one of those offshoots. You know, one of those weird vampire nights," Julie said.

"And that woman from NightTimes—" Wren began.

Mandy smirked. "Miss Pathetic of the Long Nails."

"She told us you were deep into the scene. Practically famous."

Greta, Kia realized. *They've been gossiping about me with Greta.*

"Is that why you don't hang with your music program pals anymore?" Wren asked. "Because they don't want to play vampires?"

"That vampire crap gives goth a bad name," Julie added. She shook her head. "I thought you were cooler than that."

Kia looked at her food tray. She couldn't understand how a month ago these girls were looking up to her and now they were acting as if she didn't belong in their sorority.

Mandy giggled. "So do you bite people?"

"Why? You offering me your blood?" Kia asked, narrowing her eyes and smiling what she hoped was an evil, vampire smile. "'Cause I didn't have much breakfast and I'm starved."

Mandy looked startled and leaned back in her chair. Virgil snickered.

"What's the matter, Mandy?" Kia pressed. "Too intense for little girls like you?"

Julie glared at her with a definite challenge on her face. Mandy and Wren just looked nervous.

"Unlike you goth *kids*," Kia said, "the vampires mind their own business." She picked up her tray and moved to a table populated by some freshmen. They stared, unsure of what to make of her.

She glanced up as Virgil sat down opposite her.

"Is it true?" Virgil asked. "You into that scene full-on now?"

Kia shrugged. "Why not?"

He tipped back his chair and studied her. "You tell me. You know more about it than I do."

"It's not like they say," she said, for some reason wanting him to understand what it was she saw in the vampires. "They're really nice. And it's fun. I feel . . . accepted when I'm there."

"I didn't know you didn't feel accepted elsewhere," Virgil said, not looking at her, as if he were nervous about what he was saying.

"You know how things get," she said, even though she didn't know if that was a true statement or not. "I—It's . . . it works for me, okay?"

Virgil's dark eyes now focused on her. He nodded. "Okay."

"Do you want to come with me to court?" The words startled Kia as they came out of her mouth, though by then it was too late to stop them.

"Court? Like a trial or something?" He laughed, making his dimples appear. "Are you under vampire arrest or something?"

"No, no," she responded, laughing at the image. "Court like royalty. It's a regular get-together."

"And you want to take me there?" Virgil asked.

Uh-oh. She didn't want him to get the wrong idea. "Well, I want you to see for yourself what it's like. Anything I say in its defense will be suspect, right?"

"I guess," he said.

"Sunday at eight. And it's even over at a decent hour."

"Okay, it's a date."

Kia cringed at the word *date*, but Virgil had already grabbed his books and left the table.

At least maybe now one person in the whole school would see she wasn't a freak.

Sunday night Kia met up with Virgil outside Red. He seemed apprehensive.

"It will be cool. You'll see," she assured him, ushering him inside.

Kia introduced Virgil to Osiris and Dark Star, the blood-bonded couple she had met the last time. They were just as warm to him as they had been to her.

He'll see how nice everyone is here, Kia thought, watching him talk with Lady Margaritte, who had come over to join their little circle.

Damon's party scene was for a specific type of person, she admitted, but surely *this* event wouldn't weird anyone out. Certainly not someone like Virgil.

A cold hand gripped the back of her neck. Kia flinched, but then she realized who those cold, strong fingers belonged to. She smiled and stood absolutely still.

"Hey," Virgil said to the person behind her. "Back off."

"I don't think Kia wants me to," Damon said.

Kia let out a long, dreamy sigh. She felt his lips near her ear.

"Do you want me to back off, Uptown Girl?"

Kia reached up so that she could rest her hand on the back of Damon's neck. She shivered with the reference to the night in the park, a secret they shared. He had just given her a nickname even—like real couples had for each other.

Damon moved his hand down to her hip and stepped next to her. Virgil frowned and fiddled with his pockets.

"I heard you've been getting to know the court," Damon said. "I thought I might find you here."

She grinned, unable to hide her happiness at the fact that he'd been looking for her, and then realized Virgil was still standing there. She didn't want Damon to think she was with Virgil. But she couldn't be all-out rude either.

"Damon, this is Virgil. He's new."

Damon nodded. "Virgil. I guess I can't blame you for wanting to protect Kia."

Virgil just looked at Damon and didn't say a word.

Okay, now who's being rude? she fumed, glaring at Virgil. Why did he have to look so young? So high school. Damon might be able to figure out her real age.

"So you were looking for me?" Kia asked, turning her back on Virgil.

"I can't stay. I wanted to give you this." He pulled a flyer out of his coat pocket. Another "invitation only" party at the same loft space in Brooklyn.

"Thanks," Kia said, smiling up into his dark eyes.

"Hang on," he said. He took the flyer back and scribbled something on it. "E-mail me so I know you're coming." He stepped away from her. "Got to go." He hurried back out to the street.

Kia watched him leave, wondering if she should follow him.

"That guy," Virgil said. "I've seen him at the other clubs."

"What?" she said, turning around.

"He acts like he owns you," Virgil grumbled.

"Does he?" Kia asked, smiling. Even Virgil could see how much Damon liked her.

"There's something . . . I don't know . . . *off* about him," Virgil said.

Was Virgil just jealous—or did he sense that Damon was the real deal? A true vampire?

"Come on," Kia said, leading him to a banquette. "They're going to start the ritual."

They found seats and Virgil leaned back against the velvet banquette, looking as if he were trying to disappear. Luckily, he drank the fake blood when it was offered.

"You see?" she said, once the ritual was over. "That wasn't so weird."

"Hmm." Virgil's response was noncommittal, and Kia wondered if he was only pretending that he was okay with the scene.

"Everyone here is so nice," Kia went on. "We're like family to each other. When I was upset, Osiris and Dark Star were really supportive and sweet. And we didn't even know each other."

"Do you know each other now?" he asked. "Do you know anything about anyone here, other than their taste in clothes?"

Kia felt her face grow hot. "I know what's important. That they give me support when I need it. That this is a community that doesn't judge. Not like most people I know. They let me be me."

"Do they? How much do you let them know about you, Kia?

Do they know the simple stuff, like where you live? That you're in school? Most of these people are a lot older than us."

"So?" Kia said coldly. "That's all superficial."

"Do they know that you have an amazing ability with color, that you see things that other people don't, which is why your paintings are so beautiful? Do they know that you're screwing up right and left at school? Do they know about your mom?"

"Shut up," Kia hissed. She stood up. She had to get away from him. But she didn't want to leave him behind either. She didn't want to risk that he would start talking to the vampires about her. What if he blew everything?

"I think you should go," she said.

"I think *we* should go," Virgil said, standing up.

A commotion at the front door stopped Kia. She glanced over to see what was going on.

A woman in jeans and a knit sweater pushed her way toward the center of the room. "Andy!" she shouted. "I know you're here."

"You're in the wrong place," Lady Margaritte told the woman. "This is a private party."

"Oh, I'm in the right place," the woman said, fury and disgust exploding from her. "I know he's here. I know all about this sick stuff."

"Please," Lady Margaritte said. "We want no trouble here."

"There you are." The woman stalked over to Osiris, who had just come out of the back room with Dark Star. He started at seeing her, looked around as if he were trying to find some avenue for escape, then stepped behind Dark Star, who was far too small to give him cover.

"Get away from him," the woman told Dark Star.

"You smell of the Mundane world," Dark Star sneered. "Your kind has no power here. Not over me and not over Osiris."

"Are you kidding me?" the woman said, her voice nearly a shriek. "What B movie did you get that from?"

"Kathy, please, go home," Osiris said. "We'll talk about this later."

Dark Star turned and looked at Osiris in shock. "You know this Mundane, Osiris?"

"Know me?" Kathy demanded. "We've been together for, like, five years."

Now Dark Star stumbled away from Osiris.

Kathy faced the room. "Want to know more?" she said, her eyes flashing with a bitter anger. "This guy you call Osiris? I don't know what he pretends here, but *Andy* is a computer programmer at an insurance company. Fascinating, don't you think? Really dangerous, huh?"

She took a step toward Osiris again. "This little play world is why you don't want us to live together, isn't it? And your freak playmate."

"You're the freak!" someone shouted from the back.

"Get rid of her, she's poisonous!" another person called.

"Osiris, don't let her define you!"

"Your identity is yours!"

"Take her blood," a voice shouted.

"Blood!" a few people shouted. "Blood!"

For the first time Kathy looked frightened. Kia's stomach clenched.

"We should stop this," Virgil said, taking a step.

"No," Kia ordered, grabbing his hand.

People stomped and clapped. "She's a threat!" people shouted. "Get her out!"

"This is our world." A gaunt vampire stepped up to Kathy and pushed her toward the door. "You're not welcome."

"Please," Lady Margaritte begged. "No violence."

"Our world!" people chanted, drowning her out. "Our world."

"We have to protect it! Protect our own!" someone cried.

Now the whole room was filled with shrieking, screaming vampires. *They're right,* Kia thought, *everything was fine until the Mundanes came in and ruined it.* "Our world!" Kia screamed.

"Stop!" Lady Margaritte cried above the shouting. "We don't behave this way."

No one paid attention. Kia pushed forward into the crowd and saw Kathy's face streaked with tears, Dark Star gleefully shoving her, Osiris standing on the bar clapping. For one moment Kia stood still.

They've been together for five years.

And this is their breakup.

Kathy stumbled, and one of the men near the door gripped her arm and dragged her out. A cheer went up when he turned and clasped his hands over his head in a sign of victory.

Kia frowned, suddenly exhausted. She knew they were right—she knew they had to protect their turf, keep their world together by acting together, but still . . .

Lady Margaritte sat crying at the end of the bar.

Kia turned to look for Virgil and realized he was gone.

Kia got home earlier than usual that night. After the scene with Kathy there was a big debate on how to proceed: do a cleansing ritual (Lady Margaritte's idea), have Osiris and Dark Star renew their blood-bond vows (Dark Star's idea), drink heavily (Osiris's solution), and a lot of talk about how to keep the Mundanes from destroying things.

Kia didn't have much to contribute to the discussion so she split. Her head hurt, and the boots she had worn pinched her toes.

"Kia, get in here."

Her father was sitting in the living room, and from the tone of his voice, she knew she was in trouble.

Now what?

Kia dropped her purse on the floor and sank into the chair. "I'm beat, Dad. Can this wait?"

"No, it cannot." He stood and paced. "What the hell is wrong with you?"

Kia's mouth dropped open. He had never spoken to her like that before.

"I'm sorry," her dad said. He ran his hands through his hair a few times. "Let me start over." He paced some more, then sat on the coffee table in front of her.

He leaned his elbows on his knees and stared at the floor. She could practically hear his brain trying out and discarding multiple phrases, only she had no idea what he was about to say.

He stood again. "Maggie phoned."

"Is something wrong with Mom?" Kia asked, terror pushing out every other thought.

"What? No, she called about you."

"Me? What would she have to say about me?" Kia thought about the last few weeks. She'd made visits to the apartment and she and Maggie got along fine.

"Did you think no one would find out about the fact that you've all but dropped out of school?"

Kia's blood froze.

"Your school sent a notice to the apartment. Maggie didn't want to upset your mother, so she waited until she could talk to me without her overhearing."

Of course. The school had her mom's apartment as the official address. How could she have been so stupid?

He started pacing again. "I know I've been out of town a lot." He shook his head. "Maggie couldn't wait to berate me for that. As far as she's concerned, I'm the worst father in the entire world."

Was that what he was upset about? The fact that she skipped school made him look bad? She almost laughed.

He turned to face Kia again. "I thought I could trust you," he said. "I've got so much on my plate; this case is . . . well, it's make or break for me on this case. And I've been so proud of the way you . . . And it was all a lie."

"I—" Kia started. But she wasn't sure what to say, so she decided it was safer to say nothing. Not until she figured out a strategy.

"Maggie thinks you're into drugs, into some weird scene."

"I don't do drugs," Kia said vehemently. "You can ask anybody."

"Then what are you doing when you're not at school?" her dad asked. "Where do you go? Who are you with?"

Kia shrugged. "I—I just stay here."

Her dad stared at her. "Gee, Kia. I wonder why I don't believe you."

Kia stood up. "But it's true," she said.

"Well, from now on, I'm keeping extremely close tabs on you. Maggie is going to be checking up on you when I'm out of town. No more sleeping over at Carol's or Aaron's. Oh—and your job is history."

"What?" Kia's skin crawled with horror. "You can't do that."

"Already done," her dad said. "I called NightTimes and talked to some guy named Stevo. He knows you're no longer allowed to work there."

Kia thought she might throw up. "The one thing in my whole sucky life—and you're taking it away from me."

"You proved you can't handle school and a job. That you can't be trusted. That you're not responsible."

Kia's nostrils flared. She felt like a dragon, like flames were going to shoot out of her. She wished they would.

Damon. How will I see Damon?

"Starting tomorrow, everything will be different," her dad said. His voice softened. "We're worried about you."

"No, you're not," Kia said. "If you cared about me, you'd see that this is important to me. I need to work there. I need—"

Her dad's jaw tensed. "You need to do what I tell you. You are still a teenager. My rules rule here."

"Fine." Kia stomped out of the room.

She slammed her door shut and flung herself onto her bed. Gripping her comforter, she rode the sob like a wave as it worked through her. She buried her face under a pillow, not wanting her dad to hear her cry.

She rolled onto her back and stared up at the ceiling, her face crumpling as the horrible fate sank in. There was nothing for her except that world.

She curled into a ball, then as a familiar craving stole into her body, she slammed her feet onto the floor and went into the bathroom. She watched her hand grab the razor. She lifted it—and stopped.

She looked up at her tear-stained reflection in the mirror. *No.*

She wouldn't let her father do this to her. She had control. She'd show him.

I'm stronger than this.

Kia dropped the razor and went to the computer on her desk. She logged on to the court site and posted a message under a brand-new screen name. She wanted to be careful, didn't want Damon—or anyone else—to know the post came from her.

I've had a secret for a long time, she wrote. *I cut myself. Well, I used to. I stopped, but tonight I almost did it again. My life seriously sucks and I don't know what to do about it.*

She hit send and shut her eyes.

It felt good to get it out. To state it plainly—even if anonymously.

Several posts popped up.

Well, that would be a waste of blood! We do cry over spilt blood (as opposed to milk) when there's no one there to enjoy it with you. Hang in there. J

I agree with that—you never know when you'll need it!

Darkness sometimes overtakes us. Balance is all. Let the moment be what it is, don't judge yourself, and it will pass.

Kia found herself calming down. A new post came in.

If you're into cutting, you're my kind of night creature. I'm looking for a submissive who's into kinky stuff like that. E-mail me your address and I'll be right over.

Ewww. Kia was glad she used a fake name.

The next post was from NOMAD:

We all have secrets. That's a given. Having secrets doesn't make you bad or weird; it makes you complex. And one of the most powerful exchanges is when you share secrets with others who understand you. I'm glad you posted. Maybe one day you'll let me know who you are. I've got secrets of my own.

She stared at the screen, thinking again how NOMAD's words reminded her so much of Damon, and suddenly it hit her—NOMAD was Damon spelled backward. It had to be him. But how could she be sure?

Then she remembered the flyer—Damon had written his e-mail address on it.

It was in her purse. But the purse was in the living room.

She quietly cracked open her door and listened. The light in the living room was out. Good sign. She tiptoed to the room, hoping her dad was firmly ensconced in his bedroom watching TV.

She picked up her purse and scurried back to her room. She pulled out the flyer. There it was—Damon's e-mail address.

She was right—Damon was NOMAD.

She sat hard on her bed.

Should she tell him this message came from her? No. She wasn't ready for him to learn her secret. Not yet.

But she was ready to learn his. She just had to figure out how.

FIFTEEN

Two weeks of unendurable hell. Two weeks of living in a police state, with Maggie coming over in the afternoons and her dad around all weekend. Staring at her. Trying to *relate*.

School was even more awful than usual. Virgil steered clear of her. Aaron and Carol eyed her warily.

She hoped that if she put up a good front and visited her mom a lot, Maggie and her dad would relent and let her at least go out on the weekends. She was going through serious scene withdrawal. So far, though, they hadn't changed their minds. Not even over the pitiful, depressing, painfully forced together-ness of the four-day Thanksgiving break. Dismal and phony, the so-called celebration Kia had been forced to withstand con-sisted of Maggie's traditional turkey, which no one really ate, while the ghost of Thanksgivings past hovered over every-thing—made all the weirder by the unaccustomed presence of

Kia's dad for the day. It was the first time Kia's parents had been together in one room in she didn't know how long, but between her dad's typical awkward aloofness and her mom being so out of it, it didn't really seem like any of them were actually in the same place.

Hecate kept Kia company over e-mail, but Kia was only interested in news of Damon—and Hecate didn't have a lot of info there. Kia spent most of her time catching up on schoolwork, lurking on the court web site, and thinking about Damon.

How much longer can I stand this? Kia wondered for the twenty-thousandth time. She sat at her desk working on her long-neglected art portfolio. The centerpiece was an angelic demon drawn in charcoal. It only made her miss him more.

Her computer made a small ding, and she turned right away to see the new message. She'd gotten up the nerve to e-mail Damon the day after she got jailed. Just a "hello" and to let him know she was going to be busy with stuff so she wasn't able to see him or go to the party. He e-mailed back that he'd miss her. That sustained her for a while. Then she'd e-mailed again today:

> *Damon—I read what you wrote about secrets to that girl who was struggling with cutting. I agree with you: sharing secrets is a kind of sacred bond.*

She'd been waiting anxiously for a reply for about an hour now, and so far there'd been two false hopes. But this time . . . her heart jumped when she saw NOMAD in her in box, and she quickly scanned the message.

Exactly, Uptown Girl. Where would we be without our secrets? And what can be more intimate than revealing them to someone? But you have to be ready. Are you?

She was trying to come up with a reply when there was a knock on her door. "Yeah?" she said, quickly logging off.

Her dad stepped into her room; Maggie followed right behind him. *Great. Now they're going to gang up on me.*

Maggie sat on Kia's bed. Her face looked saggy, like a basset hound's. Her dad's had a similar weighed-down look to it.

Did I do that to them? Kia wondered. The school thing was that big a deal?

Her dad cleared his throat. "Kia, we have something to tell you. It's difficult."

Warning bells clanged in Kia's head. She hoped they would be loud enough to drown out whatever they might have to say. She could tell from their expressions that she didn't want to hear it.

Maggie patted the bed. "Come over here."

Kia shook her head. She didn't think she could stand being that close to her, to anyone in this moment. If she shattered, it would be best for everyone if she kept her distance.

Maggie glanced at Kia's dad, worry creasing her forehead.

"Your mother," he said, then stopped. He looked out the window.

Okay, he had given Kia the title of the conversation. Now did he want her to read his mind? She looked to Maggie for help. Maggie looked away.

While her father seemed uncomfortable, Maggie was on the verge of tears. Looking at her more closely, Kia realized that

Maggie had already been crying. Her eyes looked puffy and her nose was sort of red.

Kia's foot began tapping a rhythm on the floor. Maggie's eyes returned, but now Kia was the one to avoid eye contact.

"Kia," Maggie said, her voice frighteningly gentle.

Kia fought hard to keep her hands in her lap, to not cover her ears and start screaming to drown out the words she knew were coming.

"Is she going back into the hospital?" Kia asked. Her voice sounded harsh, in stark contrast to Maggie's soft tones.

Maggie's sad eyes glanced at Kia's dad again. *She keeps thinking he's going to help out here,* Kia realized, a sneer stretching her mouth.

Maggie must have realized her dad was a lost cause and looked at Kia again. "No."

That answer surprised Kia. Then why were they so upset? Why was her dad afraid to talk to her. "Dad?"

"Your mother is going into a hospice instead," he replied.

"Okay," Kia said.

"Do you know what a hospice is?" Maggie asked.

Kia shrugged. "Some kind of small hospital." She tried to remember if she'd seen any ads on TV for hospices. "But more . . . homey?"

"Well, yes," her dad said. He swallowed. "But they are special because their staff is trained to deal specifically with people who aren't going to get better. So that their final days are comfortable."

Kia's ears burned; she heard a strange sound and realized it was her own blood, pounding in her head. Rushing through her.

She discovered she couldn't stop blinking. It was as if her eyes were trying to make the scene come into better focus. As if everything were blurry.

"I'm so sorry," Maggie said.

Kia nodded. *There are probably things I'm supposed to ask. I'll try this:* "When?"

"Tomorrow."

"We're going with her," her dad said. "But we don't think you should. Not tomorrow. She'll need to get settled."

"If you'd like to see her and spend time with her, that's fine. These places are designed for long visits," Maggie said. "I'll be happy to go with you."

"Me too," her father said firmly.

"If I don't go tomorrow, will I—will she . . . ?" Kia couldn't finish the question.

"They're not sure. But they think in the next month. So you have time."

Where are my tears? Kia wondered. Wasn't she supposed to be crying? She felt hollow inside, as if her tears had been annihilated.

Maggie stood. "I need to get back," she said. "I'll call you tomorrow."

"I'll walk you out," Kia's dad said. They left the room.

Kia stared at the doorknob for a little while. It was brass, with inset consecutive circles.

She swiveled in her desk chair and logged back on, clicked into the court bulletin board.

Chatter chatter chatter. About upcoming events. About bands. About what had happened at the Court of Draconia with Osiris and Dark Star.

Was NOMAD online? She didn't see his name.

She scanned the postings. A lot of the people who wrote in had standard signatures that appeared at the bottom of every post: *In the name of blood* or *Darkness reigns* or *Death into everlasting life.*

Kia looked at that last one a long time. She opened her Write Mail file and sent Damon a private message.

Damon—I've been ready longer than you know. Don't be afraid—your secrets won't surprise or frighten me. I want to know all. Let me come downtown tomorrow night and I'll prove it to you.
Uptown Girl

She hit send and leaned back against her chair.

Her mother might have to die. But that didn't mean she couldn't live on in another form.

Now all Kia had to do was get Damon to agree to sire her mother.

SIXTEEN

Kia paced under the streetlight on the corner where she was supposed to meet Damon. She was shivering with cold and anticipation. She wished she smoked because it would have given her something to do with her nervous hands.

It had been easy to sneak out of the house. After her dad came back from checking her mom into the hospice, he had a hefty scotch or two, then took a sleeping pill. *And he was worried I was into drugs,* she thought.

How should she ask? Should she just come right out and tell Damon that she knew that he was a vampire? Or should she lead up to it by telling him about her mother? About what she wanted to have happen?

Cold wind stung her skin, made her eyes tear. She angrily brushed away the tears that streaked her face, ruining her makeup. She wore the dress she had on that first day he had spoken to her in NightTimes. The one he told her she looked great in, the one that looked better on her than on Kali.

She shivered again. Where was he?

Did he chicken out?

No, that wouldn't be like him. He was just late.

She turned, and he was right there in front of her.

"Hello," he said, his breath visible in the cold brittle air.

"Hi," she said. She had to get this started quickly before she lost her nerve or got distracted by how much she wanted to kiss him, to feel his body pressing against hers, to cry and have him comfort her, to have his intense presence obliterate everything else. She couldn't let herself get carried away; she was here to accomplish something.

"I'm cold. Take me somewhere warm. Where we can get warm together," she said.

He brushed her hair out of her face. "Like a club?" he asked. She could feel him testing her.

"No." She slipped her fingers into the waistband of his leather pants. "Somewhere private."

He took a step back, not so far that she had to let go of him, just far enough for him to look at her better. He smiled and licked his lips. "I guess we could do that."

She stepped into him and laid her head on his chest. "Good," she murmured.

"I live upstairs," he said, wrapping his arms around her and steering her toward a nearby building.

He arranged this, she realized as he unlocked the door and led her up a flight of uneven stairs. Damon set it up so they'd meet right in front of his place. He wanted this too.

Damon unlocked his front door and she followed him in. "Welcome to the inner sanctum," he said, flicking on a small lamp. "I don't usually let anyone come up here."

Kia stood in a room painted deep maroon. A large mattress was on the floor, and plastic milk crates served as bookcases. Massive piles of CDs towered near a complex sound system. Leather jackets, black clothing, and candles dotted the floor. There was no sofa, no chairs. Damon shrugged off his coat, lit a candle, and stretched out on the bed.

Kia smiled nervously as she slipped off her coat. *He thinks I'm here to sleep with him.* Of course he did.

"You look . . . tasty," he said, his eyes traveling up and down her body.

Kia took a step toward the enormous bed. "I—there's something I want to tell you."

"Oh?" The candle flickering by the bed cast shadows on his face, making his dark eyes even more intense. He rolled over and lit some incense in a burner on the other side of the bed.

Kia knelt on the edge of the bed. "There's something I need you to do."

"Name it. I'll do my best to accommodate you." He moved toward her but didn't touch her.

She couldn't look at those eyes, that mouth. She wanted to forget why she was there and melt into him. But she had to stay on track.

"I—I know your secret, Damon," she whispered.

"Do you?" He looked amused.

"I do," she insisted. "And it's all right."

"Is it?" He inched closer. She could feel his breath. "I'm glad."

"It's why I'm here. Because of your secret."

"Is that why?" His hand was in her hair.

She had to say it out loud. Or else she'd never be able to continue.

"I know you're a vampire."

There, she'd said it.

He froze a moment and searched her face. Then he smiled. "And you like that about me."

"Yes," she whispered.

"Good," he said, pulling her up against him.

She let him kiss her, to let him know she meant it. She wasn't afraid of his truth. Then a thought drew her away from him. What if being sired, being turned into a vampire, was painful? She didn't want to do anything to hurt her mother.

I'll never have to lose her, she reminded herself. The cancer had already caused her mother long, constant pain. How bad could it be? How long could it take? Her mother had been in pain for months and months.

This was the right thing to do.

She knew he was waiting for her to say or do something.

"I want you to be your vampire self for me," she spoke up.

"Why?" he asked, his voice husky. He began to untie one of the lacings in the front of her dress. "Are you offering yourself as my victim?"

She put her hand on his, stopping him from undoing the next lace. "I need something else."

He looked puzzled but intrigued. "All right. I'm game. What do you want from Damon the vampire?"

Kia swallowed and pulled her hand from his because she saw that it was shaking and she didn't want him to think she was afraid. "It's not me. I want you to turn my mother."

Damon dropped his hand from her dress. "What?"

"You have to understand," Kia blurted. "She's dying. I need you to make her a vampire so that I'll still have her. So she won't be gone. Then she can live forever. Please." The words came out so quickly they ran together.

Damon retreated from her, sitting up, leaning against the wall at the head of the bed. "Okay, this has just gotten strange."

Panic made Kia's heart beat fast. Her brain reeled, trying to find a solution. If he wouldn't turn her mother into a vampire, he could turn Kia into one. He had always seemed as if he wanted to be her sire. Then she could turn her mother. They'd be vampires together. Maybe that would be even better.

She crawled toward him. "I'm sorry. I was wrong. I shouldn't have asked that."

She lowered herself so that her neck was at his mouth. "Make *me* a vampire instead."

His hands wrapped around her and he ran his tongue along her neck, then, pulling her down hard, he started to suck on her skin.

It felt incredible.

He moved under her so that she was straddling him, never letting go of her. Her back arched with the biting sensation on her neck, but then she realized he wasn't piercing her flesh; there were no fangs. He was just giving her a class-A hickey.

She broke away. "No," she said. "I mean it. Bite me for real. Draw blood. Make me a vampire. I want to be one too."

His dark eyes clouded for a moment, as if he was trying to figure out why she had stopped him. Then her words seemed to sink in. "I'm not going to do that." He slid out from under her. "That's not my . . . That's not my main . . ." He shook his head. "Not with you. That wouldn't be right."

"But I want you to," she said.

"No." He rolled off the bed and started flipping through CDs.

Kia stared at his back, then stood and flung herself into the bathroom. She paced the tiny tiled room, then perched on the edge of the bathtub. Her fingers drummed the porcelain rim. How could she make him do what she wanted?

She stood and yanked open the medicine cabinet. She pulled out his razor and the spare blades and plunged a blade into her skin, tracing her veins. Over and over.

He won't be able to resist. She had witnessed it herself—what happened to him at that party once he saw the blood onstage. His fangs just appeared.

Slice. Slice.

She started on the other arm.

Good. Slice. *Good.* Slice. He'd know she was doing this of her own free will. No guilt for him.

She'd never cut this much before. The red was blurring together and there was less and less white skin between the cuts.

But was it enough? She peered at her arms, watching the blood. She had to bleed enough to make him drink. Make it impossible for him to control himself.

Slice. Slice. Slice.

"Kia," he called from the other room. "You okay in there?"

Now.

She opened the door. He was standing right in front of her.

"You see?" she said, holding up her dripping arms. "I want this."

He stumbled backward. "What the——?"

She stepped toward him, and to prove how serious she was, she slashed again. She had to use the tops of her arms this time. She'd run out of space.

"Drink the blood, Damon. I want to be like you. I need to be like you. It's my only hope." She held her arms out to him.

"Are you nuts?"

She stood still. He sounded angry.

"It's all right, Damon," she told him. "I want to be a vampire. I *need* to be one of the undead." Then she smiled as she realized her mistake—for him to drink, it probably had to be from her throat. She lifted the razor to cut herself again.

Damon lunged forward and grabbed her arm, making her wince in pain. He yanked the razor out of her hand and flung it away, then shoved her onto the bed.

"What the hell is wrong with you?" he shouted, pacing back and forth at the end of the bed. "Why are you trying to freak me out?"

"I'm not. I'm not," Kia moaned. "I need you to make me a vampire. Why don't you understand that?" Why was he so mad at her? *Please oh please don't be mad.*

Damon stopped pacing and stared at her. "Are you serious?" he demanded, his voice incredulous. "It's a fucking game. There's no such thing as vampires."

Kia stared at him openmouthed, her arms beginning to ache, to sting. She couldn't understand what he was saying. It made no sense.

"You actually believe all this crap?" He shook his head. "What are you, a gullible kid with morbid fantasies?"

Kia's body shuddered, and then she collapsed in sobs. "It was supposed to be for my mom," she choked out, his words bleeding into her brain, understanding oozing through her, clumping and clotting inside her.

His eyes suddenly narrowed. "How old are you?" he demanded.

Kia sucked in air. "Seventeen," she admitted in a tiny voice.

"Oh, man." He grabbed his leather coat from where he dropped it on the floor and pulled out his cell phone.

Kia huddled on the bed. She didn't even try to keep from crying. What did it matter if Damon hated her now? Thought she wasn't cool? None of it mattered.

"Kali, get over here, I need your help. I screwed up with the new girl."

Kia rolled over, the sheet sticking to the blood on her arms. She could feel it trickling out of her.

Kali burst through the door a few minutes later. "Jesus, Damon, what did you do to her?"

"Nothing, I swear. She did it to herself."

"Yeah, right." Kali crossed to the bed. "Get me towels."

"He's telling the truth," Kia murmured. "It was me. I wanted . . . I was wrong."

Damon came back to the bed with two towels. Kali pulled

away the sheets, making Kia wince. She wrapped Kia's still-bleeding arms with the towels and forced her to sit up. The room spun a little and Kia planted her palms hard on the bed.

"Get her out of here. She's underage."

"Real genius," Kali said.

"Hey, you thought she was in her twenties. You invited her to the private stuff too. So don't get all haughty on me."

"Come on," Kali said to Kia. "Playtime is over."

Kali led Kia downstairs and propped her in the doorway while she called 911. "So did you do this because of Damon?" Kali asked after she hung up. "'Cause I have to tell you, he's not worth it. No guy is."

"That's not why," Kia mumbled. Then she decided it was better for people to think she cut herself up over some guy than the truth—that she had believed the unbelievable.

Kia and her father rode home from the hospital in silence. She'd been trapped waiting in the emergency room for five hours, and then they wouldn't release her until she'd been evaluated by the psych department. She had wanted them to call Aaron, or Carol, or Hecate instead of her dad, but they wouldn't do it. She was a minor, blah blah blah.

Kia stared out the side window groggily. After they tested her for drugs and she came up clean, they gave her a sedative. She figured her dad could have used one too.

When was the yelling going to start? It was almost harder waiting than just having him lay into her.

She stuck with Kali's cover story—it was all over some

guy. That was a lot easier to explain. She also told the shrink that she only wanted to scare the guy—she wasn't actually trying to kill herself. She just wanted to guilt him. The shrink bought that, which was probably why they were willing to release her.

She had no idea what the shrink told her dad, other than that she now had follow-up appointments and that "family therapy" was recommended. Her dad had probably told them about her mom going into the hospice.

Shutting her eyes, she sighed and thought about how heavy her body felt. That must be the sedative. Leaning back against the seat, she rolled her head slowly back and forth. "I thought I could do this for her. I thought it would work." She felt tears leak out of her eyes. "I thought I could save her."

Kia heard a sharp intake of breath, and she opened her eyes, remembering her dad was sitting beside her. She hadn't meant to say that out loud.

Her father took her hand and held it with both of his. "Kia."

She turned her head and stared out the window again.

The cab pulled up to their building and they rode the elevator in silence. Once Kia and her father were inside the apartment, Kia headed straight for her room.

"Kia, wait," her dad said. "We need to talk."

"I'm tired," Kia said.

"I know," her dad said. "But there are some things I need to say. Tonight."

Kia leaned against the wall.

"I'm sorry," he said.

Her eyes flicked up to his face. She hadn't expected that.

"I'm sorry," he repeated. He looked so much older than he had yesterday. But younger too, somehow. As if he were the same age as Kia.

"What you said in the taxi."

"I was dopey," Kia said. "Don't pay any attention."

"I have to. Because I think somehow you believe what you said. That in some way I don't understand you thought you could sacrifice yourself to save your mother."

Kia could feel her insides shudder as if her guts were sobbing. She steadied herself by putting a hand on the wall.

"I need you to hear me," her dad said. "Loud and clear. There is absolutely nothing you can do to make your mother better. Nothing. It isn't up to you to keep her alive. It's not possible, and more important, it isn't your burden."

"I wanted to——" Her voice broke off.

Her father stepped toward her. *If he hugs me, I'll snap in two,* she thought. He seemed at a loss, though, so he leaned on the wall next to her.

"I know you did. You do. But she would never have wanted you to sacrifice anything for her. Not school. Not your friends. Certainly not your health."

Kia nodded as she stared at her shoes.

"I—I don't know what you told the doctors, but I think you were trying to show me how much all of this has been hurting you. I'm sorry. I wasn't paying enough attention."

"That's okay," Kia said.

"No, it isn't." He ran his hand through his hair several times. "Do you know why your mother and I split up? It wasn't over a woman, it wasn't because I didn't love you. It was because I just didn't know how to be married. Or a dad. What I know how to do is work.

"I guess . . ." He was telling her too much, but she didn't know how to stop him.

"I left because I hate failing. And I was failing. Your mother. You." He shook his head. "I like things that make sense. Your mom and I—we didn't make sense. Your mother getting sick, well, that makes no sense at all. So I'm fumbling along looking for logic. And failing."

"And I'm making it all worse," Kia mumbled.

"That's not my point. It's the exact opposite of my point. If I hadn't been screwing up, screwing up in the worst way possible, I wouldn't have been picking you up at the emergency room."

"It's not your fault."

"Don't let me off the hook," he said. Then he laughed a short, hard laugh. "Maggie always said your mother let me off the hook too much. That's why Maggie and I don't get along so well."

Kia was too tired to stand up anymore. It was going to be light soon; she could tell by the change in the color of the sky. She slid to the floor. Her father joined her down there.

"Listen," he said. "As hard as this is for us to imagine, it's going to be just you and me from now on. I'm it. I never expected to be a dad by myself. But I promise I will try to figure it out."

"I'm not a kid," Kia said.

Kia's dad tugged the tip of her black hair and then released it. "You may not be a child, but you're still a kid.

You're a kid coping with things I never had to deal with when I was your age."

Kia couldn't help herself—she yawned.

Her dad laughed. "Okay, fine," he said. "We have time."

He groaned as he stood up. He held out his hand and helped Kia off the floor.

SEVENTEEN

Kia stared at the phone. She had already called Virgil to ask for help catching up on her art program projects. Now for the really difficult call: Carol.

She had wanted to call Carol ever since that night in the hospital but didn't really know how. But her dad had started on dadhood by talking to the powers that be to figure out what classes she could still pass and how and getting her this week off at home to start catching up so she could actually pass them. Still, the only way that passing thing would really be possible would be with serious help in the cramming department. Carol's specialty.

Kia reached for the phone, then went to her computer instead.

Carol, she typed. *I'm just going to cut to the chase. I know I messed up, and I know you're pissed, and I'm sorry. We need to talk, but right now the only way I won't flunk out is with major help. You willing?*

Kia hit send and let out the breath she'd been holding.

"Thank God for incompletes," Kia said, dropping her notebook onto the floor and sprawling on her bed.

Virgil glanced up from the computer at her desk. "They aren't 'get out of jail free' cards," he reminded her. "You're going to still have to do these."

Kia's stitches were at the itchy phase, and she pressed on her arms. She knew she wasn't supposed to scratch, but sometimes squeezing helped. The bandages made funky lumps under her sleeves, and she had cut all the way down to her wrists, so even under long sleeves the bandages were visible.

She caught Virgil looking at her arms. When he noticed her watching him, he looked away.

She pushed herself up and sat cross-legged on the bed. "I wasn't trying to kill myself," she told him.

"Okay," Virgil said. He turned and faced her. "Actually, I never thought that."

"Yeah." For some reason, she had a feeling that he'd understand. Even more than Carol or Aaron. More important, she wanted him to understand.

"I thought things were . . . different. Than they really were."

"It happens."

"Things got kind of blurry for a while, and I guess I went too far."

"That happens too. The too-far part. I'm not so sure about the blurry thing. I have twenty-twenty vision."

Kia threw a pillow at him. It landed on the floor. He picked it up and laid it across his lap.

"Does everyone at school know?" Kia asked.

Virgil shook his head. "Nah. They all think you had some drug overdose."

"Oh." Kia thought that over. "That's better than the truth."

"Maybe." Virgil grinned. "The stoners are all feeling really rejected. If you were into drugs, they can't understand why you weren't hanging with them."

Kia cocked her head and narrowed her eyes. "And what do people think if I'm hanging with you?"

Virgil plumped the pillow on his lap. "Don't know. Don't care."

"Yeah, right."

Now he threw the pillow back at her. "I don't."

"What I want to know is does it help your rep or hurt it? Hanging with the freak."

"You're not a freak," Virgil said. "Though my mom did call your dad for the four-one-one."

"Why?"

Virgil took in a breath. "They heard the drug thing. Remember I told you the reason I have to keep a budget—'cause they were afraid I was getting high? Which I was, but not anymore. So, I know something about going too far with things too."

"Oh."

"I don't anymore," Virgil repeated. "But it's not like I'm a prude or anything."

"It's okay," Kia said. "I'm not into altered states much these days either."

A little voice on the computer let Kia know that she had mail. Virgil glanced at the screen.

"Who's it from?" she asked Virgil.

"Hecate," he said.

Kia rubbed her face. It was hard to deal with Hecate. Word must have flown around the scene about her flipping out at Damon's, and Hecate kept sending e-mails asking Kia if she was okay.

Kia knew that Hecate meant well, but she was too associated with Damon, with the clubs. Which was precisely what Hecate was worried about. She kept apologizing for bringing Kia into the scene, asking if there was anything she could do. The worst thing about it all—Hecate had been right all along about Damon.

"She's the chick at the store," Virgil said. "The short pretty one."

"You think she's pretty?" Kia asked. A strange sensation that Kia thought might be jealousy warmed her skin.

Virgil blushed. "Well, in an unattainable kind of way."

Kia considered telling him that Hecate said he was cute too but shrugged off the idea.

"She's asked me a lot about you," Virgil said.

"You've seen her?"

"I went to the store a few times. I think she really wants to hear from you."

"I know. It's just . . . hard."

"Well, if you ever want to go over to see her, I'll go with you. If that makes you feel better."

Kia laughed. "Oh yeah. It would be for *me* that you'd go see cute unattainable Hecate."

"Shut up," Virgil said, but he was smiling.

•   •   •

"Kia, Carol is here," her dad said the next evening, popping his head into her room.

"Okay," Kia said. Just the sound of Carol's name made her feel sick with nerves. They hadn't spoken in, well, months. Not really. Carol had replied to Kia's e-mail with a brief *Okay,* so Kia had no clue what to expect.

She heard Carol's footsteps in the apartment, and then Carol reached Kia's doorway. She hovered in the doorway, uncertain, looking as nervous as Kia felt. Her hair was shorter, Kia noticed. And redder.

"Hey," Carol said.

"Hey," Kia replied, and looked away. How could she fix this? She wanted things the way they used to be. Simple and clear. But that wasn't possible.

"So," Carol said.

"Yeah."

Carol sat on Kia's bed. Then she popped back up again. "I am so mad at you," she said. "And I don't know what to do about it."

"I don't either."

"You just vanished!" Carol said. "Into some weird place and you wouldn't let any of us . . ." She shook her head. "You seriously screwed up. Screwed me up. Aaron too. And I'm not going to just let you slide."

Kia opened her mouth and then realized she wasn't feeling defensive or angry. This was Carol—direct, angry, and not treating Kia like a fragile nut job.

"You screwed up too," Kia said. "You acted as if you knew everything, knew more than me about what would help me. You vanished too."

Now Carol's mouth hung open. She frowned, thinking, then smiled. "So we're both screwups."

"Yeah," Kia said. "I guess we're more alike than we're different after all."

Carol sat back down on the edge of Kia's bed. "I still don't get the vampire thing," she said. "Don't get pissed, but it's just way out there."

"Not for everyone," Kia said. She lay on the bed next to Carol and looked up at the ceiling. "It doesn't have to be. I just kind of made it that way."

"Oh."

Kia glanced at the back of Carol's head. Should she tell her? About the cutting? Stop keeping that secret?

"I—" Kia stopped. No. The secret had been carried for too long. Maybe later. Maybe after these new tracks had healed, she could tell Carol and Aaron. Once it was really in her past.

Carol turned to look at her. "What?"

Kia shook her head. "Nothing. It's just there was other stuff too. Things you and Aaron didn't know about. It made things . . . harder."

"We figured," Carol said. "We're not stupid, you know." She sounded mad again.

"I never thought that, I swear."

Carol nodded.

"So is Aaron ever going to forgive me?" Kia asked.

"He's always been less mad at you than me. I think he's kind of waiting to see what I do."

"So he's on your side."

"You kind of put him there, after that scene the two of you had."

"I guess." Kia smirked. "Maybe I should do a magic spell to get you both to like me again."

Carol laughed. "Aaron's not so into that anymore. Now he's into getting on a reality show."

"He could be his own reality show."

"That's what I told him," Carol said. "So watch out, he bought a video camera."

Kia laughed, cringing. "Oh my God, that's dangerous. Thanks for the warning."

Carol stroked the bedspread. "He made me promise to call him after I saw you. To see if we wanted him to come over later." She didn't look at Kia.

"That would be cool," Kia said. "Later."

Carol flopped down so that she lay stretched out next to Kia. "I wish . . ." Her voice trailed off. She shut her eyes. "I wish a lot of things."

"Me too," Kia said.

Kia felt every muscle in her body tense as she walked into Spin, a dance club on the far West Side. She halted in the doorway, making several people bang into her.

"Go in if you're going," a man behind her ordered.

"Come on," Virgil said, guiding Kia out of the way.

Kia's eyes automatically flicked to find the DJ, her chest tight with fear. Then she looked down and stared at her shoes.

Kia had managed to pass her finals, and winter break was

now in full force, so her dad had given her permission to go out with Virgil. With a 1 a.m. curfew.

Things were definitely different.

Kia had never been afraid in a club before. She didn't like it.

Virgil must have guessed what she was feeling.

"Don't worry, I pre-screened for vampires," he said. "And I brought these along, just in case." He pulled two cloves of garlic from his pocket. "Can't be too careful."

Kia burst out laughing.

"Excellent reaction," Virgil said.

"Did you know that you have dimples?" she asked.

Now he blushed. "Well, yeah. They're kind of right there on my face."

"Did you know they're cute?"

He blushed harder and looked away. "Want something to drink?"

"Sure."

Kia followed him toward the bar. The place was crowded, with no particular scene in force. Goths mixed with preppies mixed with arty-cool neighborhood types. Not a fang in sight. Virgil had done his homework.

"Kia!"

Kia turned and saw Hecate. Her feet stopped moving.

Hecate hurried toward her and stepped in as if to hug her, then stopped herself. She looked uncertain. "So, what's up?" she asked cautiously.

Kia shrugged rather than say anything. Seeing Hecate brought it all right up front.

"Look, if you want me to back off, cool," Hecate said. "But I want you to know . . . I'm really, really sorry about getting you into that scene. I never would have if—" Hecate shook her head. "Well, you know."

"Yeah. I—I don't blame you," Kia said. "You tried to get me out before I got so in."

"One of the few times I wish I wasn't right," Hecate said. "But you're here. You're looking good."

"Things are okay." Kia smiled. "Getting there."

"I heard about your mom. Sorry."

Kia nodded. Virgil must have told Hecate that her mom had been moved into the hospice. It was getting a little easier to visit there—her mom was obviously being well taken care of, and there were family counseling groups that Kia sometimes dropped in on.

A powerful dance beat pounded out of the speakers as the song changed. Hecate grinned and started to move her pelvis to the rhythm. "Well, one thing's for sure. The music never did anyone harm."

"True."

Hecate tipped her head toward the dance floor. "Shall we?"

Kia allowed the driving drum and bass lines to enter her body. "I think we shall." They wove their way through the gyrating bodies on the dance floor.

Kia shut her eyes, feeling the power, the pulse, shaking out the fear, shaking off the past, releasing all the tension inside her through the music. *Let it all go,* a voice said in her mind. *Leave it all behind on the dance floor so that you don't have to carry it around with you anymore.*

She opened her eyes and smiled at Hecate. Hecate looked happy, sharing this moment of abandon with a friend.

Kia danced closer to Hecate and together they found a groove, laughing as they tried to outmaneuver each other. They giggled like giddy kids, stomping together and apart. They banged into people around them, but no one seemed to mind.

"There you are," Virgil said, appearing behind Hecate. He had a glass of soda in one hand, wine in the other.

"Here you are too," Kia said. She took her drink and tried to not spill it as she continued to move with the beat. Virgil smiled, nodded at Hecate, and knocked back his Coke.

"I give up," Kia said, nearly pouring her red wine down the front of her dress. "Here, take this," she said, handing the glass to a girl walking by. The girl looked confused, then shrugged and walked away with Kia's drink.

Kia spun around and around, letting the music fill her up so that there was no more empty space inside. She whirled to face Virgil again, who was moving from side to side in time to the music.

"I don't believe it!" she exclaimed. "Virgil is actually dancing!"

"Okay, now I believe anything is possible," Hecate joked.

"Not *anything*," Kia said. She grabbed Hecate's hand and they danced in a ring around Virgil, who was now moving in ever stranger and more dramatic ways.

She shut her eyes again and could feel Hecate and Virgil near her, connected to her. Kia realized she could talk to Hecate about her mom. Hecate was older; she'd been through stuff. And she didn't know Kia's mom, so she wouldn't be sad about what was happening the way Carol and Aaron were. Hecate could probably even handle hearing about the cutting, which Kia was on the cusp of sharing with Virgil too. Now, though, she thought she might be able to let it out with dancing, with words, with painting. At least she would try.

She grinned at Virgil. He continued to dance dramatically.

"What do you think?" he asked, kicking his legs like a Rockette.

"Now you're scaring me," Hecate said, doubling over, laughing.

"Oh, I don't know," Kia said, forming a kick line with Virgil. "I think there's hope for you yet."